The Mostly True Story of Pudding Tat, Adventuring Cat

THE MOSTLY TRUE STORY OF PUDDING TAT

ADVENTURING CAT

CAROLINE ADDERSON

Illustrations by Stacy Innerst

GROUNDWOOD BOOKS
HOUSE OF ANANSI PRESS
TORONTO / BERKELEY

Published in Canada and the USA in 2019 by Groundwood Books

Groundwood Books / House of Anansi Press
groundwoodbooks.com

We gratefully acknowledge for their financial support of our publishing program the Canada Council for the Arts, the Ontario Arts Council and the Government of Canada.

With the participation of the Government of Canada
Avec la participation du gouvernement du Canada | Canadä

Library and Archives Canada Cataloguing in Publication
Adderson, Caroline, author
The mostly true story of Pudding Tat, adventuring cat / Caroline Adderson ; illustrations by Stacy Innerst.
Issued in print and electronic formats.
ISBN 978-1-55498-964-5 (hardcover).—ISBN 978-1-55498-966-9 (EPUB).—
ISBN 978-1-55498-967-6 (Kindle)
I. Innerst, Stacy, illustrator II. Title. III. Title: Pudding Tat, adventuring cat.
PS8551.D3267M67 2019 jC813'.54 C2018-903795-4
C2018-903796-2

Illustrations by Stacy Innerst
Design by Michael Solomon

Groundwood Books is committed to protecting our natural environment. As part of our efforts, the interior of this book is printed on paper that contains 100% post-consumer recycled fibers, is acid-free and is processed chlorine-free.

Printed and bound in Canada

This book is in memory of Sheila Barry,
the first to believe in this little cat.

Parasitism: The relationship between two living things in which one of them — the parasite — lives off a host.

Symbiosis: The relationship between two living things in which both help and benefit each other.

CONTENTS

1
WELLAND COUNTY, ONTARIO, CANADA
1901

THIS is the mostly true story of Pudding Tat, much-traveled cat, whose adventuring life began in the first year of a new and promising century. Not ours, but one long ago.

Pudding was born in a hayloft where the heat from the horses and cows rose and warmed the night. To the lullaby of laughing whinnies and quiet, sweet-breathed moos, his mother added her contented purring. Mother Tat was so pleased with her latest batch of kittens. Two black, one gray, one tabby, and the curious white one she called Pudding.

Pudding Tat. Through the years he would stand out in many ways, but most obviously for being the color of the dessert he was named after — milk boiled with sugar and a pinch of salt, with cornstarch to thicken it. The special treat that Farmer Willoughby brought to the barn on Christmas Day every year.

For more than a week Mother Tat's helpless kittens wriggled beside her, blind, deaf and toothless, their mews silent. Then at last they opened their watery eyes and looked around the dim old barn on the Willoughby farm.

In this, Pudding was different, too. His eyes didn't open. Even so, he was the first of the squirming, nuzzling kittens to attempt to stand. No sooner had he got up on all fours than one leg trembled and gave way, and he toppled back into the hay. He didn't give up. He tried again on his four white wobbly legs.

Eventually, he succeeded. They all did, and grew sturdy.

Soon they were tumbling over each other, taking a few daring steps away from Mother Tat before rushing back. They were not very brave — except for Pudding. Despite his closed eyes, Pudding would wander away from Mother Tat and just stand there listening to the captivating sounds of the world. The buzz-huff-hum-twitter-thrum-scratch-squeak.

"Open your eyes, Pudding," Mother Tat urged.

He could open them now, but preferred not to, which was strange. They were beautiful eyes, as pink as his tongue. His brothers' and sisters' eyes, meanwhile, had changed from blue to green or amber.

During the day, the sun would beam through the cracks around the hayloft doors, revealing the dust and spider tapestries and long hammocks of cobwebs. Then Pudding would blink violently and shrink back. At night he was more comfortable, but he still couldn't see well. He recognized the black void that marked the edge of the hayloft, but he couldn't tell how far away it was.

How would he ever catch mice, Mother Tat worried when the kittens were ready to learn. She was an excellent mouser. An excellent teacher, too. While she'd been nursing her kittens, the mice had taken advantage of the peace and produced their own babies. Mice that were just peaking in plumpness and overrunning the barn.

This was how Mother Tat went about their lessons.

First, she killed a mouse herself and divided it into five equal parts to give the kittens a taste of fresh mouse meat. Other than their special treat at Christmas, the barn cats never ate human food. From their very first taste they longed only for raw mouse — bone-in, with the fur still on it.

Next, Mother Tat lined up her kittens in the hay. She caught a mouse, then opened the trap of her jaws. Off it shot, the kittens bounding after it. Pudding, too, though he was always in the rear, following his brothers and sisters.

One kitten got hold of the tail, but the mouse jerked free. They swarmed it.

"Very good," Mother Tat cried. "Well done!"

The mouse escaped. Mother Tat caught it again and divided it up as a reward for her five talented children.

After a few days of this, Mother Tat began to tutor each of her kittens separately. All of them progressed more or less as well as her previous litters. Except for Pudding. Without his brothers and sisters to follow, Pudding used a different method. He couldn't rely on his eyes. Instead, when Mother Tat released the mouse, he sat and listened.

Mother Tat wondered why he was giving the mouse a head start.

"What are you waiting for?" she asked.

There. Pudding picked out the sound he needed. A tiny mouse heart beating. He dashed for it but, misjudging the distance, ran straight into the hayloft wall. The mouse escaped. Pudding rubbed his stinging nose with his paw.

It pained Mother Tat to see Pudding fail like this again and again. He was hopeless! If he couldn't catch mice in the barn where they were plentiful, how would he manage in the wide world? Would he even get the chance? A fox would spot a white cat a mile away. Or he'd fall into the river and drown.

But she kept these fears to herself and, hoping for the best, continued to encourage him.

Hunting was just one skill Mother Tat taught her children. They would need so much more if they were to survive. She taught them the signs of an approaching storm: red-sky mornings, aching bones.

She taught them never to walk behind a horse, but always in front. She'd lost her own brother, their Uncle Tat, when he was kicked by a startled plow horse. She taught them not to go anywhere near cart wheels, or the long blade of Farmer Willoughby's scythe. She showed them the scythe hanging on the barn wall — a terrifying implement that smelled of oil and new-mown hay.

Stay away from humans altogether, she warned. Just in case one had a sack tucked inside his coat. She'd learned from her own mother, who had learned from hers, about farmers loading kittens into a sack for drowning. Yes, they drowned kittens if they thought there were too many cats in the barn.

Her favorite lesson, though, was when she taught them to wash. How delightful to see all five Tat kittens in a row, their pink tongues combing their fur. This was the one thing Pudding was good at, so Mother Tat made sure to praise him for it.

"Between the toes, like Pudding. Between the toes."

Thanks to her guidance and love, the kittens thrived. Their legs got leggy and their tails got taily. They were always clean. Now they hunted everything — mice, spiders, the swallows that plastered their mud nests against the rafters of the barn. (They did not have much success with swallows.) They hunted each other. They were mighty hunters of the Great Race of Tats!

Soon they were confident enough to leave the loft and go exploring. Pudding, too, went bumbling after them.

"Go. Take chances," Mother Tat told them as she shooed them out. But to Pudding she always whispered, "Be careful."

The whole barn was theirs to explore now. The kittens leapt from the loft's sudden edge to a shelf in the milking parlor, from the shelf to the top of a stall, and from the stall to the floor. Pudding fearlessly followed his brothers and sisters by scent and sound. If it was night and safe to open his eyes, he trailed behind their shadowy forms.

Mother Tat, watching from above, prayed that Pudding would keep up. He usually did. To himself, he was Fearless Pudding the First.

One morning the barn door squawked open while the kittens were exploring. Farmer Willoughby tromped in clanking his metal pails. Four of the five hunters immediately scampered back to the loft, leaving Pudding behind.

Someone else entered the barn as well. It was the smaller Willoughby, his son, Johnny. He saw the kitten marooned on a post. Hard to miss a white cat.

Johnny got his father to squirt some milk into

his cupped hands. Then he took it to Pudding while Mother Tat watched from above, desperately calling out.

"Run, Pudding!"

Instead, Pudding began to lap the milk from the boy's hands.

Little Johnny Willoughby shivered in amazement. The barn cats were wild. Normally they would hiss and bare the fierce needles of their teeth if Johnny even came close.

But this white one was different.

Gently, so as not to startle the kitten, Johnny touched the top of the white head. The kitten pressed against it as though he wanted Johnny to pat him. Johnny stroked the silky length of his coat. Stroked and shivered again.

The kitten's mother was crying frantically from the loft, so Johnny stepped away and watched the kitten leap from the post to the shelf, then from the shelf to the hayloft.

With closed eyes. How did he do it?

At the end of a long night of exploration and play, Mother Tat would call her kittens to her. Then they curled together in a patchwork heap — tabby, black, gray and white — to hear her stories.

She told them about their formidable Grandfather Tat the Thirty-Seventh, who had walked out of the barn one morning. He had traveled to the four corners of the wide world. This was hard for Pudding to picture since he had yet to leave the barn himself and could only see a few feet in front of his face.

In fact the cats' wide world was only the Willoughby farm — the farmhouse and its outbuildings, the surrounding fields and woods, the stream that flowed on to the Niagara River, and the neighboring Welland County farms. There really were four corners where the rough country roads intersected and marked the boundaries of the farm. Mother Tat told them that was where the carts passed, with their cat-crushing wheels.

Beyond the farm was a stream that any water-hating cat would refuse to cross, including Grandfather Tat. That was where he had stopped.

"Is that where they drown the kittens?" one of Pudding's siblings asked.

Mother Tat said that, sadly, any water would do for that awful purpose.

"How long was Grandfather gone?" the less-fearful Pudding asked.

"Years and years," Mother Tat said.

Mother Tat paused to look at her heap of children, so innocent and dear. They weren't kittens anymore.

Would she ever see them again, her precious ones, once they left? So few cats returned. They would find homes of their own in other barns or in the woods. This was the best she could hope for. The worst was some fatal mishap with a scythe or plow, a fox or yard dog.

In all cases, their leaving was a mother's sorrow.

One day while the Tat cats were napping in a pile, a mouse chanced into the hayloft. The kittens woke the instant they smelled it. Mother Tat, too. She wanted to watch her children in action, to be absolutely sure they were ready to go.

The mouse, likewise smelling the cats, realized its mistake just as the five kittens sprang out of the hay. It ran straight over the edge of the loft, twisting in mid-air as it fell. It bounced off the soft back of the chestnut horse in the stall below and onto the straw-strewn floor. From there it darted to safety.

The kittens followed in a stampede. Three stopped at the loft's edge to watch the falling mouse. Pudding, who misjudged the nearness of the edge, didn't, and neither did his black brother, who was running too fast to stop.

The falling kittens were not as lucky as the falling mouse. They missed the horse's back completely.

Pudding landed first on his four white feet, as cats do. His brother came crashing down on top of him. Because Pudding had broken his fall, his brother leapt away unhurt.

But the horse, already spooked by the mouse, kicked out with his hind legs and sent Pudding flying through the air a second time. They all heard the terrible sound of Pudding's soft body striking the barn wall.

Mother Tat let out a yowl. In three bounds — from the edge of the loft to the shelf in the milking parlor, all the way to the barn floor — she flew. Fearlessly she darted under the slashing hooves and snatched Pudding by the scruff.

When she returned to the loft with his pale limp body, the other kittens circled her, bawling. Mother Tat laid Pudding in the hay.

She said, "Children. Look at your brother. He got behind a horse."

As the kittens cried, Mother Tat washed her strange white child and hoped he would survive.

For some time before this accident, a change had been taking place in the barn. A change so gradual that no one noticed it but Pudding.

Someone was singing.

Oh, the flea jumped on the dog
And drank his blood, hey ho!

Before long, several other voices joined in.

From cat to dog, from dog to horse, from horse to cow,
He drank their blood, hey ho!

Then hundreds of voices sang.

These were the fleas, which, like the kittens, were born (hatched out of eggs, actually) at regular intervals in the barn. Just as the lives of the cats and mice were connected, so too were the lives of the cats and fleas. They even shared part of their name. *Felis domesticus* and *Ctenocephalides felis*.

As each flea was born, it joined the party on the backs of the barn cats, where it drank enough blood to get drunk. Drunk, it sang and danced.

All the cats began to itch and scratch. But only Pudding, whose hearing was exceptionally keen, could hear their bellowing laughter and rowdy conversations, the same jokes over and over.

How do fleas travel? They itch-hike!

After the chestnut horse spooked and sent Pudding flying into the barn wall, he woke to the same flea hullabaloo as before. His frantic mother was washing him. His brothers' and sisters' frightened meowing added to the din of the singing. He put both paws over his offended ears.

For several hours he lay like this, curled up in the hay and blocking his ears as he recovered from the blow. Because he was not up and about with his brothers and sisters, there was nothing to distract him from those tuneless songs. They grew unbearable. "The Bloodless Flea's Lament" went on for hours.

Woe to the flea who has no blood,
Not a drop of blood to drink!

Pudding longed for the buzz-huff-hum-twitter-thrum-scratch-squeak again. The purr-mew-nicker-clank. The rustle-sigh of the wind.

Then Pudding heard a brash and bossy voice. "You planning on lying here forever?"

Pudding sat up. He stuck his back foot into his ear and scratched.

"Hey! Cut it out!"

"Who's there?" Pudding asked.

"It's me, your mother," answered Mother Tat, who had not heard the flea. She hovered worriedly over Pudding. "Don't you recognize me?"

His brothers and sisters came running, too, but

Mother Tat shooed them off. Curling up beside Pudding, she resumed her devoted washing.

"I got a good one for you," Pudding heard from somewhere on his back. "What do you call a cheerful flea?"

From directly inside Pudding's ear came a grousing reply. "*Bor*-ing! I heard that joke about a zillion times!"

"A hoptimist!"

"Shut up, already!"

Those were Pudding's sentiments exactly.

"You're not going to croak are you?" the voice asked.

Pudding scratched again.

"Hey!"

"Who are you?" Pudding asked.

"Someone who's sick of living with this gang. I saw you covering your ears. I'm guessing you're sick of them, too."

"I am!" Pudding said.

"Well? Why don't you ditch 'em?"

"How?" Pudding asked.

Mother Tat paused in her washing. Pudding's mutterings made her whiskers tremble and her mother's heart beat with alarm.

"Who are you talking to, Pudding?"

"I don't know, Mother," Pudding said.

"Vamoose," the voice said. "Let's go."

Pudding knew they would soon be leaving the barn. Mother Tat had prepared them for that day all their lives. A new batch of kittens was coming. It was time for them to set out as independent cats.

They would all leave together, of course. Not only was Pudding accustomed to following his brothers and sisters, but with fleas drowning out the most important of his senses, he depended on them.

But when the day came, Mother Tat took Pudding aside. Since his accident, her doubts about his survival had only increased.

"I'd like you to stay a little longer. I want to make sure you're all right."

"I'm fine. I'm ready," Pudding told her. "The voice says it's time to go."

"Don't tell her that!" the voice roared.

"What voice?" Now Mother Tat was truly frightened. "Pudding, dear? You're in no condition to leave. Wait here while I see your brothers and sisters off."

As soon as she was gone, the voice said, "What are you waiting for?"

"I have to say goodbye. She's my mother."

"So?"

Over the parasite party, Pudding heard his brothers and sisters tearfully begging to stay.

"You're Tats," Mother Tat told them. "Strong and brave."

It was only her mention of the farmer's sack that convinced them in the end. If they didn't leave, there would be too many cats in the barn.

"I love you all!" she cried, before returning to the loft.

"About this voice, Pudding?" she said. "Don't listen to it."

"Don't listen to *her*," the voice said. "Aren't you a Tat, too? Strong and brave?"

Yes, he was! More than that, he longed to be like Grandfather Tat and visit the four corners of the world.

Then the barn door squawked and opened. Hearing the clank of the pails and little Johnny's chattering, Mother Tat fell silent.

Johnny told his father, "The white one is my favorite. He always comes to say hello."

Pudding, seizing the moment, leapt from the edge of the loft.

"Goodbye, Mother!"

He landed on the shelf in the milking parlor, then jumped down to the straw-strewn floor as well any seeing cat. He'd done it a hundred times.

"Stay!" Mother Tat cried.

"I'll be back!" he told her.

This only made Mother Tat cry harder.

"See?" Johnny said to his father. "I told you he'd come."

But before Johnny knew it, the little white cat had slipped out the barn door and was bounding up the path, the flag of his white tail held high.

Johnny set down the pail. He was about to go after the cat, but his father put a hand on his shoulder.

"Chores first, son. Feed the horse. Take the milk up to the house. Then you can play with the cat."

Farmer Willoughby settled on his stool and reached under Betsy, patient and brown. Milk streamed rhythmically into the pail.

By the time it was full and Johnny was toting it with two hands up the path, legs wide, trying not to spill, the cat was long gone.

HOTEL LAFAYETTE
2
+ NIAGARA FALLS, ONTARIO, CANADA +
1901
Mrs. Annie Edson Taylor
Heroine of Niagara Falls

As he left the barn, Pudding Tat could hear his mother's faint cries over the racket of the fleas, but he didn't turn back. The wide world drew him on from the moment he stepped outside. The farm, the woods, the fields. He smelled it all.

And something else. His sensitive whiskers tingled with it.

Change.

The wide world was changing. Like Pudding, people were on the move, leaving farms for the cities, the old world for the new. Some wanted a better life, others adventure. All of them were dreaming. Dreaming big — of automobiles and airplanes, subways and electric lights. Dreaming of the things we take for granted now, but which were new amazements then.

The voice urged him on. "Giddy-up."

"Who are you?" Pudding asked.

"We're looking for water. Find some. Quick."

Pudding, eyes closed, moved through the confusion of odors. Hay freshly cut and waiting in the fields. Windfall apples softening in the orchard. Finally his nose picked out water. He ran for it.

Straight into the side of a trough.

"What the —" said the voice. "Why'd you do that?"

Pudding rubbed his stinging nose with his paw. "I found water."

"We need more than this. We need a lot of water. A body of water."

So Pudding moved on until his next collision — with the split rail fence around the pasture. He slipped under it into a harvested field where the left-behind stubble pricked his paws.

"Wide world" meant vast. Now that he was out of the farmyard he sensed it. And he remembered the stories Mother Tat had told him about Grandfather Tat. How he'd reached the first corner of the world, rubbed himself against it, then carried on.

Pudding was following in his formidable footsteps!

Before too long the footsteps bumped him into something else. A tree. Though he didn't know it, he'd reached the woods dressed in the golden finery of fall. He began to pick his way through it.

Somewhere, there would be a stream. Mother Tat had talked about it.

When he lifted his head to sniff, he realized that night had fallen and he could open his eyes. He'd only ever seen the sky through the hayloft window. Now it spread above him, full-mooned, milky with stars, lighting the way painlessly for him.

All this time the flea party was still going on.

Where do fleas shop? At the flea market!

And the voice in his ear kept complaining, "Boring, boring, boring ..."

Soon Pudding grew hungry. Mice scurried out of his way, uncatchable without walls and corners to serve as traps. He was cold now, too, and lonely. He'd never been alone in his whole life. Already he pined for the barn and that cozy, thrumming pile of cats.

"Why're you stopping? You can't stop right out in the open with foxes all over the place."

Not alone.

"I miss my mother," Pudding said.

"Keep moving. We need water."

"Water," Pudding remembered and plodded on.

"Atta boy."

After a minute, Pudding thought to ask, "Why are we looking for water?"

"We're going to drown these good-for-nothings."

Drown? How cruel the voice sounded now. *Bloodthirsty*.

Pudding stopped again. "Who *are* you?"

"A flea," the voice said. "What did you think?"

Now is the time to tell you about Pudding's traveling companion and how he, too, was different from his kin. Just as mannerless and bloodthirsty, yes, but unlike the hundreds of other fleas cohabitating with him on Pudding's back, he wanted to improve his life.

The flea, too, was born on the Willoughby farm. Born from one of six hundred eggs his mother had laid in the hayloft. Unlike Pudding, he wasn't nourished from his mother's body, not washed and warmed and taught how to survive. The flea's mother simply laid her eggs and went on guzzling blood. If the flea ever clapped eyes on her, he wouldn't even have recognized her.

Worse, once he'd hatched, not as a flea yet, but a larva — wiggling and white, like a worm with hair — his mother still didn't bother with him. She didn't even feed him. And what he and his brother and sister larvae had to eat was almost too disgusting to mention.

They ate the poo of the adult fleas.

During his time as a helpless larva, the flea experienced neither tenderness nor encouragement. He heard not a single kind or well-mannered word. No one spoke to him at all. Instead, he wriggled through the hay, blind and legless, fighting over poo with his hundreds of siblings while the adult fleas danced and drank and utterly disregarded their parental responsibilities.

Finally, the time came to make a cocoon. No one taught the flea how to do this. He had to figure out on his own what the sticky thread coming from his rear end was for. He wrapped himself in it until he was swaddled in a muffling sack.

Now at least he could fall asleep and forget the awful life he'd been born into.

His five hundred and ninety-nine brothers and sisters also spun themselves cocoons, but unlike this flea, they were eager to become adults so that they could start living a dissolute life — drinking and dancing and singing, not giving a hoot about anything or anybody. They fell easily to sleep, pupated for as short a time as possible, then kicked their way out of their hastily spun cocoons and joined the party.

Pudding's flea tossed and turned. It was so noisy! He squeezed out a little extra silk and stuffed his ears with it.

Finally, he fell into pupation, which was so much better than being a larva that he wanted to stay in his cocoon forever.

But in the end, he had to rejoin his family. It was Nature's way. He emerged wiping the sticky threads off the six legs he'd grown while asleep, finding everything as before. The same unruly conversations, the same dumb jokes, the same four-hour ballads. Jumping and dancing and blood glugging.

No one even noticed he was back.

His new body was covered in bristly armored plates — hard, flat and brown. His moustachy mouthparts hung down. Each segmented leg ended in a pair of claws. He tried to squeeze out some more silk for earplugs but had lost the knack.

What could he do now but dance and jump and drink blood?

He didn't want to do those things. He believed he was destined for a better life.

So, though on the outside he was hideously identical to every other flea, inside, this flea was very different. He saw that he had a choice of hosts. Pudding was the one he picked, for he noticed how this cat followed the others, as though obeying them. Several times he saw Pudding cover his ears.

Did he, too, hate those endless flea songs?

He sprang on the white body and made his way through the fur forest on Pudding's back and settled in his ear. From there he started on his plan for personal improvement.

"You're a flea?" Pudding said. "Then aren't these your brothers and sisters singing on my back?"

"Yep," the flea replied.

Pudding remembered Mother Tat's stories about kittens snatched and stuffed in sacks and how he and his siblings curled tighter together to keep each other safe.

"You want to drown your own brothers and sisters?"

"As soon as possible." He began to yell insults at the other fleas. "Drunks! Poo-eaters!" To Pudding he said, "Don't get me started."

Wanting to drown your own relatives seemed cold-blooded to Pudding. And it was. A flea is an insect and insects have cold blood.

"Giddy-up," the flea said.

"What if *I* drown?" Pudding asked.

"Better not," the flea told him. "A dead host isn't any good to me."

Pudding walked through the night in search of water. What drove him on was the thought of hearing once again the buzz-huff-hum-twitter-thrum-scratch-squeak, the rustle-sigh of the world.

The stream was there, but too far away to smell. Unbeknownst to him, Pudding was walking parallel to it, straight toward the mighty Niagara River.

At dawn the sun peeped over the horizon, blinding him. Under his feet, the ground sloped into a shadowy basin, making a perfect place to rest after his all-night walk.

Cats need sleep — a lot of sleep.

The smell of water was so close. But it would be there, too, when he woke up.

A few miles from where Pudding had curled up in the ditch stood the luxurious Lafayette Hotel — five brick stories with a turret overlooking Niagara Falls.

Every room in the hotel was fitted with modern conveniences — electric lights, hot and cold running water, a flush toilet. There was even a museum in the lobby showing photographs of the falls, arrowheads and clay pipes and other historical curios, as well as stuffed birds and animals.

Recently a special display had been added — the oak barrel in which Mrs. Annie Edson Taylor, the "Heroine of Niagara Falls," would take her death-defying plunge later that morning.

No one had ever attempted such an impossible-to-survive feat. To be carried along with the six hundred thousand gallons of water that coursed over the falls *every second*, then plunge 167 feet straight down into the swirling Niagara River. In a barrel! It would be smashed to bits. *She* would be smashed to bits. Then she'd drown. The best thing that could happen was her heart would give out.

She may as well go down in a coffin.

At that moment, though, the heroine was still alive in her bed, sobbing into her pillow while her manager, Mr. Russell, pounded on her door.

"Annie! Get up!"

"No!"

"I'm coming in. I've got a key."

"I'm not dressed!"

"Then get dressed!"

Mrs. Taylor had no choice. With a despairing sigh, she climbed out of bed.

Was this really the day? She hobbled over to the window, drew back the heavy drapes and looked down at the furiously cascading water. She heard its ceaseless din along with her own imagined screams as she went down.

All week hotel boys had peddled advertising handbills to the tourists strolling along the terrifying edge of the falls. *Annie Edson Taylor Takes the Plunge!* Thousands were expected to line River Road to watch her die.

She shuddered and let go of the drapes. For a few moments she distracted herself by pushing the buttons on the wall and watching the magic show of electric lights. How the glowing bulb was connected to the falls outside, she couldn't fathom, but Mr. Russell said that was where the electricity came from.

"Annie!"

"I'm washing!"

The wonders of the modern world continued in the water closet. When she pulled the chain on the cistern above the toilet, a miniature Niagara Falls appeared inside the bowl.

If only she could flush herself down the toilet instead!

In the mirror, the face she washed, framed by long gray hair, seemed to have grown older overnight.

Mr. Russell rattled the handle.

"I'm getting dressed!" she called.

She pulled on her woolen underpants and her stockings, squeezed into the corset and hooked it tight so she might actually fit inside the barrel. Strapped in like this, she felt calmer. She laced her boots and put on her new dress — black satin for a widow and a soon-to-be corpse.

Then Mrs. Taylor put her hair in a bun. All the newspapers would be there. She wanted to look presentable when, dead or alive, they pulled her out of the barrel.

At last she opened the door to a furious Mr. Russell. Even his moustache, waxed into sharply curled points, looked angry.

"Ready," Mrs. Taylor told him. With great dignity she hooked her arm through his so that he could escort her to that other wonder, the elevator, and down to the dining room.

They put out a sumptuous spread at the Lafayette Hotel. As this was likely her last meal, Mrs. Taylor planned to stuff herself as much as the corset would allow.

You may be wondering what drove Mrs. Taylor to attempt her plunge.

It was desperation.

After decades as a dancing teacher in far-flung towns — from Sault Ste. Marie to San Antonio to Mexico City — she'd had to retire. She was crippled by bunions and corns — bumps and lumps all over her feet. At sixty-three, she was an old woman for that time.

Where could an old woman with no family go? In those days it was to the county poorhouse. The old, the sick and the penniless got a bed there and some slop to eat. It was hardly better than a prison.

The previous year, Mrs. Taylor had passed through Niagara Falls. She hadn't stayed at the Lafayette Hotel, but in a cheap boarding house for tourists. One night at dinner another lodger told how he'd accidently dropped his cigarette case over the falls, then hurried down to the base and actually found it washed up there. Mrs. Taylor, whose feet throbbed terribly that night, listened to the story with great interest.

Several months later, in another boarding house in another town, she met Mr. Russell, a talent manager with traveling acts. Bearded ladies, conjurers and sword swallowers were his usual clientele.

She told him her idea, and the next day he produced a contract.

Until a few days ago she'd been pleased with how Mr. Russell had arranged everything — the fancy room at the Lafayette, the publicity, the speaking tour that would follow her plunge. Even a new dress!

But as the deadly day drew near and she began to lose her nerve, Mr. Russell became more and more impatient with her.

That morning, as they stepped out of the hotel, Annie gasped at the sight of the crowd lining the promenade. Mr. Russell grabbed her arm and bustled her along, knocking her feathered hat askew. The cart that would convey them to the drop-off spot upriver was waiting there for them, the barrel in the back painted with the words MRS. ANNIE EDSON TAYLOR, HEROINE OF NIAGARA FALLS.

She gripped Mr. Russell's arm. "I don't want to die."

How easy it would have been for him to say

something kind. He could have told her that everything would be fine. Even if he didn't mean it.

Instead he hissed, "You should have thought of that before."

So Mrs. Taylor, who was a brave person, a survivor who had rallied her spirits that morning to face the day's events, began to slump again.

Outside town the road followed alongside the river, which babbled happily without giving any hint of the dramatic plunge ahead. Mrs. Taylor looked out at the fields stubbled in gold.

Would she ever see fields again, or take a breath of autumn air?

Once she'd had a family — a husband and a baby. But the baby had died and Mr. Taylor, brokenhearted, had run off to be killed in the Civil War, leaving Mrs. Taylor to fend for herself.

Would Mr. Taylor be waiting for her in heaven? Would she recognize him if he was? It had been more than forty years since she'd seen him.

All her life she'd tried not to think of the baby. It was too painful. But now a thought came to her. If Mr. Taylor was there, would he have the baby with him?

She turned her head so Mr. Russell wouldn't see her tears. As she did, something caught her eye. Something in the ditch.

"What's that? Driver, stop."

The carter pulled the reins. Mr. Russell leaned over Mrs. Taylor to see what she was pointing at.

"Some kind of animal. It's dead."

Mrs. Taylor shivered, then roused herself to defy the omen.

"How do you know? Let me see."

As she stepped down onto the road, Mr. Russell exploded. "No more stalling, Annie! We're already an hour late!"

Mrs. Taylor ignored him. Lifting her black skirt, she skittered down into the ditch — ouch, ouch, ouch. Her bunions would kill her if Niagara Falls didn't.

"Why, it's a cat!" she cried.

When she touched the cat, she felt life under her hand. Drowsily, the animal lifted its head. Its eyelids fluttered but didn't open.

Pudding had been sleeping soundly until that moment. The flea's attempts to rouse him had had no effect. Not yanking on his ear hairs, or screaming over the general commotion.

But Mrs. Taylor's touch woke him up.

"No, no, no!" the flea roared as she picked up Pudding.

Mr. Russell slid over on the seat, making a space between him and the cat. Under his curled moustache his lips pursed with disgust.

"Drive on," Mrs. Taylor told the carter.

She inspected Pudding from nose to tail. Satisfied that he was unhurt, she began to stroke him.

Pudding enjoyed this very much. It reminded him of the boy in the barn who fed him warm milk from his cupped hand. But each time the huge looming hand came down, the flea shrieked.

"Aren't you beautiful?" she murmured to the cat. "Aren't you precious?"

"Isn't this the pits?" said the flea.

With the cart rocking back and forth, the horse's rhythmic clops and the melodious river rushing past, Mrs. Taylor felt moved to sing.

I love you truly, truly dear,
Life with its sorrow, life with its tears,
Fades into dreams when I feel you are near ...

Competing with Mrs. Taylor's singing were the drunken fleas.

Don't give him water, don't give him tears,
It's blood that feeds the flea.
Hey ho! Hey ho! Blood feeds the flea!

Pudding had heard the flea singing so often that he didn't really hear it anymore. But he'd never heard real music until now. It was as beautiful as the buzz-huff-hum. The purr-mew-nicker-clank. The rustle-sigh.

He was entranced.

As she sang, Mrs. Taylor's thoughts turned to her baby. He'd weighed so little. As little as this cat. He'd been nearly as pale, too. In fact, the cat's mews reminded her of her baby's sickly cries. And now the grief that she'd held in her heart all this time came pouring out.

"Again?" Mr. Russell said. "You produce as much water as the falls."

Goat Island came into view in the middle of the river. They stopped at the spot where they'd chosen to launch. Mrs. Taylor climbed down with the cat and stood blotting her eyes while the men lifted down the heavy barrel and rolled it to the riverbank.

"Precious," Mrs. Taylor whispered Pudding's ear.

"Gag," the flea said.

"Give me that cat and get in," Mr. Russell said.

But now Mrs. Taylor felt brave again. She certainly wasn't going to hand the cat over to Mr. Russell. Instead, she tucked him under her arm, pulled out her hatpins and gave Mr. Russell her hat.

"Just in case I make it," she told him.

If she didn't make it, she could accept death now.

She would meet that little baby again, she was sure. Why, he'd be a grown man. Imagine that!

She set the cat on the ground, made a shooing motion, then got down on her hands and knees. Inelegantly, due to the tight corset, she backed into the barrel. She had to push hard to get her rump in, but the oak staves widened in the middle and she fit.

The moment Pudding's paws touched the ground, the flea began to yell his head off for him to run. The river was right there. This was their chance.

But Pudding didn't run. He stood waiting for Mrs. Taylor to sing again. When she looked out of the mouth of the barrel and saw the cat still there, she clicked her tongue and beckoned to him.

"No, no, no!" the flea roared, pointing with four pairs of claws toward the river. "Right over there? That's water!"

Mr. Russell had gone back to the cart for the lid. He returned in time to see the cat step daintily inside the barrel. He clamped the lid on anyway and tightened the screws.

Inside the barrel, the warbles of the drunken fleas and the protestations of the sober one sounded even louder to Pudding. The barrel began to roll. They heard a splash. Mrs. Taylor shrieked.

"What did I tell you?" the flea said. "Water."

Bob and swirl, bob and swirl. They picked up speed, clipping rocks. The terrified passengers — human, animal and insect — were jostled and jarred. The top of Mrs. Taylor's head knocked against the lid but was protected by her bun.

She clung to the cat, screaming, "My baby! Oh, my baby!" while Pudding struggled uselessly.

Hey ho! Hey ho! sang the oblivious fleas.

The crowd lining River Road was growing restless. Many had decided it was all a prank and gone for lunch instead.

Then someone with opera glasses cried out, "There it is!"

The barrel was just a speck at that distance, falling too fast now and too far.

Down,

down,

down,

down!

It hit the bottom and disappeared. The spectators held their breath.

"She's a goner," the man with the opera glasses said.

The barrel popped back up, miraculously whole.

Waiting at the base of the falls were the newspaper reporters and photographers and two men hired to retrieve the barrel. The men leapt into the waiting boat, rowed out and snagged it with a hook. They already knew that Mrs. Taylor had survived by the screaming coming from inside.

They towed the barrel to shore, rolled it up the bank, then set to freeing the hysterical heroine.

The second they got the lid off something white shot out.

"What was that?" asked one of the reporters.

Pudding raced in a blind circle, around and around until he tumbled down the bank and landed in the water again.

The men shrugged and returned to extricating Mrs. Taylor, who seemed to have swelled from the trauma of the ride. In the end it took two of them pulling on her arms and a third sitting on the barrel to liberate the now-famous lady.

She was completely dry, but her hair was a mess.

While this was happening, Pudding was in the river paddling in desperate loops, each moving him closer to shore.

Water! That kitten-drowning substance. To think he had been seeking something so awful. He clawed his way up the bank and for a drenched moment stood there, shrunken-looking, more like a white rat than a cat. His beautiful fur pasted to his scrawny body, he sneezed and coughed and shook himself.

"Atta boy," came the voice of the flea.

The only flea left.

Two days after her historic plunge, Mrs. Taylor's nerves were still shot. She had yet to leave her room, let alone begin her speaking tour in the Lafayette Hotel museum.

Mr. Russell grew even more furious. Every day that they didn't sell tickets, they lost money.

Mostly Mrs. Taylor slept. Pudding, too, curled up in the bed with her. He was more traumatized from his plunge in the Niagara River — the icy water touching his skin and filling his lungs — than the ride down the falls.

And now the falls roared on just outside the window, reminding him of his terror and drowning out the mostly flealess silence he might otherwise have enjoyed.

The single happy creature in that room was Pudding's remaining flea.

"Eat," he encouraged Pudding when a meal tray was brought to Mrs. Taylor. Pudding fed on the tidbits she gave him — boiled eggs and buttered toast, roast beef and Yorkshire pudding. He barely tasted them.

The flea did, second hand, smacking his shaggy mouthparts. Pudding's blood was rich and roast-beefy now instead of thin and mousey like before. Within a day he'd drunk so much of it that, like Mrs. Taylor, he'd swelled.

"You did good, kid," he told Pudding. "I had my doubts there, especially on the way down. 'Shoulda picked the tabby,' I said to myself."

The Lafayette Hotel was something else as well. As he drank Pudding's tasty blood, the flea looked around at the velvet curtains and the rose-garden wallpaper.

Of course! No wonder he'd been unhappy. He belonged in a place like this, not in a dingy old barn. He was a higher class of *Ctenocephalides felis*. Not like the other washed-away, poo-eating riff-raff. Better looking, too!

"Not only that. Do you hear it? No, you don't. Because there's *nothing* to hear! We got rid of those bums! Ah, silence ..."

Pudding put his paws over his ears to shut out the roar.

3
+ BUFFALO, NEW YORK +
1901

On the third night after their plunge, Pudding woke and began to wash Mrs. Taylor's face. He wanted her to sing again. The unbearable roar outside the hotel window was wearing down his nerves.

Instead she clutched him to her chest and sobbed all over him. Fearing another wetting, he wriggled free and began to wash himself. As he washed, he pondered how to escape. He was ready to set out again in search of the four corners of the wide world.

Meanwhile, Mr. Russell had also come to a decision. He was Mrs. Taylor's manager, but in a way he was a parasite, too, like the flea — a man without special qualities of his own who made his living off other people. His moustache even resembled a flea's shaggy mouthparts.

Though he'd arranged for her historic ride down the falls and her speaking tour, as a parasite, Mr. Russell was concerned only with himself. It wasn't long before he realized that he didn't actually need Mrs. Taylor. The barrel would do. With it beside him, he could describe her thrilling descent and her sad nervous collapse. Without Mrs. Taylor, Mr. Russell could keep their entire share of ticket sales. He'd earn twice as much!

That night, while the night clerk slept behind the desk, his head resting on his folded arms, Mr. Russell and the carter simply carried the barrel out of the hotel and loaded it into the waiting cart.

Then Mr. Russell had another idea. Animal shows were the most popular. He'd probably earn *three times* as much with the cat.

He went upstairs and snuck into Mrs. Taylor's room. The frazzled heroine was snoring in her bed with the cat beside her, washing himself. Easy to see in the dark.

The first stop on Mrs. Taylor's speaking tour was Buffalo, where the Pan-American Exposition was attracting thousands of visitors every day. The cart drove to the railway station on the New York side of the Niagara River, the stolen barrel rolling around in the back, Pudding and his flea tossed about inside it. Pudding meowed with terror. He didn't want to get wet again.

So it was a relief when the barrel was finally lifted down and set somewhere solid. Nowhere near water as far as Pudding could tell. They were far from that roar.

"How are you going to get us out?" the flea demanded.

"I don't know," Pudding said.

"You have to *do* something," the flea said. "*Doing* is what the host is for. That's you, buddy."

In a way, a single voice echoing in the barrel was worse than the chorus of hundreds, for it was personal, addressed to him. What a boob Pudding was to get them in this situation, the flea told him in his brash, rude voice. The Lafayette Hotel was just the place for a high-class flea like him. They had to go back. Right this instant!

Very faintly, in the pauses between these complaints, the sound of birds worked its way through the oak staves. Dawn had broken. Pudding hadn't heard the birds so clearly for a long time. Soon a soft swishing and another kind of twittering — whistling — reached his sensitive ears.

Then footsteps.

Someone had opened the barrel before. Maybe they would again. Pudding meowed.

Mr. Russell's plan had been to take the first train and be gone before Mrs. Taylor woke. Since they'd reached the station in plenty of time, he paid a visit to the gentlemen's room. There he massaged fresh wax into his moustache and shaped their tips into new curls. He took a tin of tooth powder out of his case, rubbed it on his yellow teeth with his finger, spat it out.

When he was finished, he smiled at the mirror for giving back such a handsome picture of himself.

By the time he returned to the platform, several other passengers had gathered. The porter was there, too, to help the passengers board and to load their luggage. At the moment, he was whistling as he swept around the barrel.

"When's the first train, George?" Mr. Russell asked him.

No one called porters by their real names back then. They called them "George," after the man who owned the train company, George Pullman.

The porter, whose actual name was Asa Philip, hated to be called George. There were other things about the job he disliked. How his weekly wage, already low, was docked to pay off his uniform. How he had to get to the station early every morning to sweep, though he wasn't paid for this chore. How he could never hope to rise to the position of engineer.

But being called by your rightful name was to every man, woman and child a sign of respect. The wide world was changing in this way, too. *Everyone*, not just the Mr. Pullmans, deserved respect. So whenever anyone called Asa "George," he would simply offer a courteous correction, as he did now with Mr. Russell.

"It's Asa."

"I didn't ask your name," Mr. Russell said. "I asked when the train goes."

"The Pan-American Express departs at seven-twenty," Asa told him.

Pudding was still meowing, trying to get someone to let him out of the barrel.

"Sir?" Asa said to Mr. Russell. "There's a cat in this barrel. Do you think it has enough air?"

"Sure it does," Mr. Russell answered. "If it didn't, it wouldn't be yowling like that."

With these words came a terrible rumble, followed by the screech of metal on metal, agonizing to Pudding. Then train station bustle.

No passengers were disembarking. They were all on their way to the Exposition in Buffalo.

Asa helped them board.

"Name's Asa, ma'am, sir," he said, over and over.

He returned to load the heavy barrel.

MRS. ANNIE EDSON TAYLOR, HEROINE OF NIAGARA FALLS.

Asa saw the bold white letters. An avid reader of left-behind newspapers, he knew about Mrs. Taylor's plunge. Here he was, carrying the famous barrel to the baggage car on his strong back!

He set it in the corner. The poor cat was still crying, so Asa tapped out a jaunty rhythm on its lid.

"You just hang in there, Mr. Cat. I'm coming back."

Eventually Pudding heard the cry of "All aboard!" and the painful screech of departing wheels. The clacking accelerated and the car began to pitch and sway.

The flea carped on.

"This barrel is the pits! I want a bed!"

Pudding meowed and meowed until he heard Asa again.

"I'm coming, Mr. Cat! I'm a coming!"

Asa unlatched the wooden lid and peered down into the dim, sour-smelling prison.

"White!" he exclaimed, whistling a descending note of surprise.

The barrel was too tall to reach the cat crouched at the bottom, so Asa shifted the bags around and tilted it on its side. When Pudding crawled out, Asa scooped him up.

"Why, you're a dandy, Mr. Cat. But what's wrong with your eyes?" He thumbed one open, causing Pudding to squirm. "Pink eyes! You are one special cat."

Asa settled on a trunk with Pudding in his lap. In a mournful voice, he began to sing.

I may be blind an' cannot see
But I'll meet you at the station
When the train comes along.

"You can't see me, can you, Mr. Cat? Not with your pretty pink eyes closed like that. But why do you have to ride in that barrel? Why can't your mistress hold you? You're doing fine in my lap."

Pudding was purring madly now, for Asa's singing voice, though deep, was as beautiful as Mrs. Taylor's. Asa, too, felt pleasure sharing this moment of rest with this beautiful cat. In a quarter hour he'd be George again.

"George Pullman doesn't own me," he muttered. "All he owns is the part of this uniform I haven't paid off."

Mr. Pullman's picture hung in the station office. Asa imagined him now, showing up in person and calling him George.

"If he did that, Mr. Cat? You know what I'd do?"

In his mind, Asa stepped right out of his pants and handed them to a shocked Mr. Pullman. "'Here,' I'd say. 'These are all that belongs to you.'"

He let out a soft whoop of laughter just as the door opened and another porter said, "Here's the baggage car, sir."

Mr. Russell stepped inside. He'd decided to check on Pudding in case the porter was right about the air in the barrel. A dead cat wasn't much use to him.

There it was, alive in the porter's arms.

"George!" he roared out. "Unhand that cat!"

Recognizing the voice, Pudding struggled to escape, but Asa held him tighter. The anger Asa felt a hundred times a day sparked up inside him. Not just for himself now, but for the poor mistreated animal in his arms.

"It's Asa," he told Mr. Russell.

"Unhand it, I said!"

Asa obeyed, lifting the crying cat back into barrel and setting the lid on top. He noticed the writing again.

Funny, he hadn't seen any woman with Mr. Russell. Not at the station nor in his compartment.

"Does Mrs. Taylor know her cat is crying?" he asked.

Mr. Russell turned such a boiled shade of red at the mention of Mrs. Taylor that Asa knew something wasn't right.

Occasionally, he caught a supposedly fine gentleman filling his pockets with Pullman silverware. Whatever passengers stole, the porter had to pay for. So Asa, not able to accuse the fine gentleman directly, would instead say, "I'm afraid the Pullman

Company doesn't offer complimentary cutlery." He'd stand firm until the man's pockets were unloaded again. And then he wouldn't get a tip.

Now Mr. Russell smiled. It was the same horrible, yellow, moustachey smile he'd given the mirror in the gentlemen's room.

He reached into his jacket pocket.

"Do we agree, George, that you've never seen this barrel or this cat?"

"It's Asa, sir."

"Pardon?"

"My name is Asa."

The cat was yowling louder than ever. Mr. Russell took some bills from his wallet.

"Here." He fluttered the money.

"Mr. Asa Philip, actually," Asa said.

"Here you are," Mr. Russell said.

Asa began to whistle. The cat stopped wailing.

"Asa ..." Mr. Russell's face pinched up. "Philip."

"Mr."

"Mr."

Asa snatched the money and stepped past Mr. Russell so that he could open the door for him.

"I never saw the barrel nor the cat. I'll let you know when we reach Buffalo, sir."

Mr. Russell fumed out of the baggage car and back to his compartment, both relieved that he'd sorted out this glitch and peeved that it had cost him ten dollars.

Well, he'd soon get the money back a thousand-fold.

Once Mr. Russell was gone, Asa left, too. Best not to go back into the baggage car until they reached Buffalo. There were several curves coming up in the track, and Asa had only set the lid on the barrel, not fastened it. Quite often the bags were in disarray when they reached the station.

He counted the money. Four times what he earned in a week.

"George! You don't even own my pants now!"

Asa laughed and knocked a little tune on the baggage-car door to say thank you to the cat.

In Buffalo, another porter came to unload the baggage. Pudding had already climbed out of the toppled barrel and picked his way through the bags.

The moment the door opened, Pudding, whose ears were still throbbing from the screech of the brakes, shut his eyes against the stronger light and ran. He landed on the crowded platform. Among the swishing skirts and striding legs, he was kicked along, right out of the station where the morning sun glared down.

Now he had a destination — away from these feet and out of the light.

He followed a wall until he reached the dim sanctuary of some bushes. Every inch of him felt bruised, but at least they were finally out of the barrel.

But did his flea offer thanks? Had he helped Pudding find his way under the burning sun?

No, but that's how it is with parasites. Me, me, me.

Under the bush, Pudding washed his aching self.

"Yesterday, a silken bed. Today a crummy bush. What a come-down!" the flea moaned.

Pudding was starting to be able to tune out the flea the way he used to tune out the whole party. He trained his ear beyond the hubbubbing station and listened hard.

Soon, his whiskers began to tingle.

Next to the bush was a high wall and, beyond that, the most intriguing assembly of sounds. They came from the Pan-American Exposition, the showcase for all the marvels of the new modern world.

What did Pudding hear? The clicks and whirs and *di-dah-di*s from the Machinery and Transportation Building where the latest inventions were on display — the electrograph, the telautograph, the wireless telegraph. The wails of tiny babies kept alive in the Infant Incubators. The gasps of the fairgoers as they took these wonders in.

"I wanna go back to the hotel," the flea said. "If not that last one, something just as posh."

More sounds floated over the wall. Pudding picked out different languages now. Spanish, Hawaiian, Swahili. These came from the model villages. Then — oh joy! — he heard instruments. Marimbas, ukuleles, drums.

A train chugged out, another chugged in, obliterating the music temporarily. Then the faint strains of an orchestra started up in one of the bandstands.

Much closer, a tinny melody — part bird, part whistle, part bell.

The melody stopped. Dragging steps approached and something heavy was plunked down, releasing a long reverberating note.

A very dirty boy crawled under the bush and flopped onto his side. Pudding's ears pricked up. There was something musical, too, in the boy's sobs.

Giancarlo Casali couldn't help but cry beautifully. He came from a musical place, a town an ocean away, Laurenzana, in Italy. In his family — they numbered fifteen with Nonna — everybody sang. They *ninna-nanna*ed the babies, warbled arias while they worked, and on Sundays fluted like angels in church.

But Giancarlo was far from his family now. Though just one of the many leaving the old world for the new, he was younger than most.

Curious, Pudding crept closer to the source of the sobs. He couldn't see Giancarlo, but now Giancarlo saw Pudding. He sniffed until his tears dried up. Slowly, so not to startle the cat, he reached out.

The flea took one look at the grubby hand coming down and shrieked in disgust. "Run!"

Pudding didn't. In fact, when Giancarlo sat up, Pudding climbed into his lap. Briefly, the boy's tears resumed because this was the first kindness visited upon him since he had come to America a month ago. This cat was the first living thing to pay him any attention, not counting the scolding attention of his padrone.

"Listen to him blubber," the flea moaned.

"*Gatto, gatto,*" Giancarlo murmured as he stroked Pudding the way the Willoughby boy had, and Mrs. Taylor, and Asa, too. "If you only knew how much trouble I'm in."

In a sing-song whisper, Giancarlo began to spill out everything that had happened to him. His trip across the pitching ocean. How for ten days he'd lain in a dark berth far below deck, groaning with seasickness. How he only stopped throwing up when he saw Signora Liberty standing in the harbor.

Many years before, Giancarlo's father had been sent to New York to sing and grind the organ in the street. When Giancarlo turned thirteen, the family arranged to send him, too. This was what was done in Laurenzana. The eldest boys were apprenticed to the padrone who came home every three years to sign new contracts.

But there were laws against street musicians now. Instead, Giancarlo would work with the crew digging up roads for the subway, the railway they were building under the city.

"Yes, a railway *under* the ground," the padrone told them. Giancarlo would earn even more there.

Already small for his age, Giancarlo arrived in New York weak from the voyage. He spent three days with the subway crew hauling the heavy buckets of dirt, or trying to.

Then the padrone threw his hands in the air.

"Useless! Never mind the laws. I can see you're good for nothing else. I'll send you to the big fair in Buffalo."

He took the boy up to the attic of the tenement on Crosby Street where Giancarlo and five other boys slept on a straw mattress on the floor. Out of a dusty pile of junk, he pulled a carved wooden box with a leather strap and one leg.

A barrel organ. The padrone stood Giancarlo behind the instrument and, slinging the strap around his neck, showed him how to balance the organ on its leg and turn the crank. Music poured out.

"Sing," the padrone said.

"I don't know this song," Giancarlo answered.

"Make up the words. Nobody can understand you anyway. Your father used to sing, 'Fat lady your nose is so big. Give me all your money.' They loved it! He earned the most of anybody."

Giancarlo didn't think he could insult people to their faces like that. His father must have been very hungry to do it. Since arriving in America, Giancarlo's stomach hadn't stopped growling. Also, he didn't feel like singing. At home he never stopped, but here in America he hadn't so much as hummed.

The padrone remembered something then. "No, the boy who earned the most was the boy with the monkey." Grinders with animals were always the most popular.

"Monkey?" Giancarlo asked.

A very disobedient monkey whom the padrone had long since sold. But now he went out and bought it back. Then he put Giancarlo on the train with the furious monkey shrieking in a carpet bag.

When he arrived in Buffalo, Giancarlo opened the bag with much trepidation. The monkey leapt out, baring her fierce yellow teeth. Somehow Giancarlo was supposed to dress her without letting those teeth sink into his flesh. He lifted out a frock and held it over her head.

Before he realized that he'd dropped his end of the leash, she scampered off, straight over the wall, the leash snaking after her.

"*Gatto,*" the boy told Pudding. "I've been turning the crank for two days, turning and turning. Because I owe the padrone my train fare and my food and lodging and the passage on the ship. I can't go home until I pay him back. And now I owe for the monkey, too."

You can probably guess what kind of person this padrone was. Fifty percent of all creatures that live on this earth are parasites.

Giancarlo told Pudding, "I have to get inside and find her. For that I need twenty-five cents. But no one is listening to me. Look. This is all I have."

He pulled a few grubby coins from his pocket. Pudding smelled the metal of the coins, the dirt and sweat on the boy's hand, and his fear. He licked the hand.

At that moment, Giancarlo got an idea. It was a terrible idea. As soon as he thought it, he began to mutter an apology over and over, "*Mi dispiace, mi dispiace.*"

He crawled out from the bush with the cat under his arm.

"Now, run for it," said the flea. "Go!"

Pudding might have, but the boy was holding

him as though his life depended on him.

Giancarlo went and stood by the station door. The arriving fairgoers streamed past. In Italian he called out, "Twenty-five cents! A beautiful cat! Just twenty-five cents!"

Pudding tucked his face under the boy's arm to shield his eyes. Several people stopped to pat him. One elderly man reached into his breast pocket and drew out a monocle on a string so he could get a better look.

Something fell from his pocket. Quickly, Giancarlo covered it with his shoe. The man moved on.

Giancarlo already knew that a cat who listened so attentively — as though he understood every word — was no ordinary creature. Here, under his scuffed shoe with his stockingless toe poking through, was proof of something else.

A ticket.

The white cat was bringing him luck.

For two days Giancarlo had seen the ecstatic expressions of the departing fairgoers. Now, as he handed over the ticket and stepped inside the gates of the Exposition, he understood.

He had entered a grander world. It spread before him like a dream. A vast plaza lined with ornate buildings. A sunken garden with a bandstand. A lacy tower so tall it scraped the sky.

Beyond, as far as he could see, were spires and domes and colored flags.

How wondrous it seemed to an undersized homesick boy. How much more so to a tiny full-of-himself flea. All this pomp and majesty spread out just for him! Every pavilion he saw as a hotel. A hotel with a huge soft bed. With room service.

He could almost taste that roast-beefy blood again.

"Yes! This is the place!" he crowed.

But perhaps the most amazing thing about this vista was what they couldn't see.

It wasn't real. Though the buildings were life-sized, though they appeared to be made of marble and stone, they were only plaster and chicken-wire constructions. By winter they would vanish. It would be as though the Pan-American Exposition had been a dream.

Pudding heard the medley of invention, music and language more clearly now. Animal sounds, too. What could this be but one of the wide world's corners?

In fact, Pudding wasn't far wrong. The Pan-American Exposition was the whole world squeezed into 350 acres. He squirmed to get down, eager to start exploring. But the boy was still gripping him. Instead Pudding made himself limp and hung over his arm, waiting for his chance to jump.

Though Giancarlo was supposed to be searching for the runaway monkey, he'd already forgotten it. Swept along in the stream of Sunday-dressed toward the bustling Midway where the cries of the barkers overlapped, he fell into a trance of astonishment.

"Step right up, step right up! Come see the Esquimaux Village!"

"A Trip to the Moon!"

"Living Esquimaux!"

"A once-in-a-lifetime opportunity!"

"Ride the Aeriocycle! Ride it in the sky!"

"*Gatto*, am I dreaming?" Giancarlo asked.

He tilted back his head and watched the Aeriocycle turn its passengers like a whirligig. Before he managed to believe what he was seeing, the crowd pushed him toward another marvel — a woman's sleeping face on a pillow three stories tall.

This was Dreamland. You entered through a door in her neck and, Giancarlo presumed, dreamed the Exposition with her.

Next he passed the Infant Incubators, where he could pay to see tiny living babies squirming in glass boxes. Before this invention, these babies, born too early to survive, would have died. Now their grateful mothers allowed them to be put on display.

Next came the many-roofed pagoda of the Japanese Village. Then the Confectionery.

He stopped to watch an apple-cheeked woman turning the crank on a machine. A broad pink skein of taffy stretched and spun.

"Saltwater taffy! Straight from Atlantic City! Taste this famous treat!"

Around and around the candy went, pink as the woman's cheeks.

It had been a long time since Giancarlo had tasted *caramella mou* or anything sweet. In his imagination he almost felt it sticking to his teeth.

"*Ragazzo!*"

Giancarlo swung around.

"I knew it! I knew you were *Italiano*!"

Giancarlo had already seen so many astonishing sights, but here was the most astonishing of all. An arcade like at home with a stripe-shirted gondolier standing under one of the arches smoking a cigarette. He waved Giancarlo over.

"Welcome to Venice in America!"

"They brought Venice here?" Giancarlo said. "The city of canals?"

"Yes," the man told him.

"How?"

"These days they can do anything. You're a disgrace, *ragazzo*. Come. Wash that mug of yours." He pulled Giancarlo through a disguised door in the wall.

Now Giancarlo really did find himself in a dream. His dream of home. He descended the steps beside where the gondolas launched and, tucking the cat under one arm, squatted to wash his face in the dream canal that was somehow filled with real water.

This was Pudding's first opportunity to jump. The flea urged him to. "Take me back to where we saw those hotels!"

But Pudding smelled the water and was afraid of landing in it.

A singing gondolier came along steering his boat with his long oar. "*La Biondina in gondoleta. L'altra sera g'ho menà!*"

Under Giancarlo's arm, Pudding perked up to listen.

"What are you carrying?" the man asked. "A cat?"

Giancarlo cupped some water in his hand for Pudding to drink. "Yes, he's my lucky cat."

The man barked a laugh. Giancarlo climbed back up the steps, and the man promptly snatched the cap off his head and swatted him with it.

"Listen, *ragazzo*. I'm going to tell you what will really bring you luck. Go to the Temple of Music at four o'clock today. The president is visiting."

"What president?"

"McKinley, *idiota*. The President of the United States. In America, anything's possible. Even an urchin like you can shake the president's hand. Even your cat can. Then you'll write home to your mother and boast. You've already succeeded so well in America that you've met the president. Go! Go!"

Giancarlo turned, but the man said, "*Ragazzo*, wait. Shake my hand first. Because maybe *you'll* grow up to be president. In America, you never can tell."

Giancarlo grinned. He held out his hand, clean now. Pudding, sensing a safe opportunity, leapt unseeingly into the air.

He tumbled down the set of stairs and nearly did end up in the water. But he picked himself up and ran in the opposite direction until his whiskers brushed a wall.

A corner? Not yet. He could hear Giancarlo far behind, calling, "*Gatto! Gatto!*"

There was just enough space for a cat to squeeze between the two buildings, but not a boy.

"Atta boy," said the flea. "Give him the slip."

In the shadows between the Children's Building and Venice in America, Pudding listened. The happy shouts of children filled his ears, but also unhappy sounds. Those of the animal captives in Bostock's Zoological Arena, directly across from where he crouched.

"Go back to where we started," the flea said again.

Instead Pudding ran straight into the parade of

feet. Like in the train station, he was kicked all the way to the other side.

Behind the false front of Bostock's Arena was an enormous circus tent. Pudding slipped under the canvas and found himself in a place dim enough that he could open his eyes. In cages lining the outside of the arena, animals panted in the heat. Visitors moved around them as at a zoo, gawking through the bars.

"Hey, lazy! Move it," a boy said. He took his mother's parasol and inserted it through the bars to goad a dispirited zebra.

The zebra huffed. A hyena whined. An incensed monkey shrieked.

Then Pudding heard a sound that made his fur stand up.

It was the roar that lived in his blood, a roar from the past, long before there were *Felis domesticus*, before there were any Tats to count.

He crept along the circular enclosure, past the camel, the peccary and the emu, until he came to the half dozen cages that housed Bostock's pride of twenty-four lions.

The old king, still lushly maned, had long ago been subdued by the whip. He rested his dejected head along his paws, too depressed even to wash himself. To anyone with a heart, this was a sad sight. To a cat it was a horrifying.

"This place stinks," the flea said. "Get me out of here."

Pudding retraced his steps out of Bostock's Arena, walking as though in his sleep. But the Exposition was no dream to Pudding. To be caged and humiliated was a nightmare. Worse than being trapped in a barrel. Worse even than the scythe, the hungry fox or the drowning sack.

The first safe place he came to was the lily garden. He crawled deep into the foliage, becoming a patch of white indistinguishable from the flowers.

In this sweet-smelling sanctuary, he set to dreaming away what he had seen.

After hours of searching, Giancarlo sank onto a bench next to a fountain. The Exposition was a crowded maze. He'd never find his lucky cat again, let alone the monkey. Two creatures lost! In despair, he buried his face in his hands.

With his eyes covered, Giancarlo experienced the exposition the way Pudding did. He heard it. The distant barkers, the laughter, the competing strands of music from every pavilion and attraction.

And from somewhere close by, the deep, sonorous notes of an organ.

He lifted his gaze. Opposite where he sat was a blue-domed building with a long line of people stretched before it.

The Temple of Music? It had to be!

Giancarlo washed again in the fountain, more thoroughly this time, to make himself presentable to a president. Face, neck, behind his ears. He combed his wet fingers through his hair, then hurried over and got in line.

By then, Pudding had woken from his nap and was washing, too, among the lilies. He heard the same irresistible strains from the organ.

"Wrong direction," the flea said when Pudding set out to follow the music. "Hello? Are you even listening? The hotels are thataway."

So beautiful and complicated! The organ was a tapestry of sound. The flea kept harping, working himself up to a conniption, until he saw the Temple of Music with its fluttering flags and its blue dome encrusted in gold.

The most majestic hotel so far.

"Yes, here!" he shouted. "I'm home!"

Inside, President McKinley had just welcomed the two thousand seated spectators. Now he turned to greet the hundreds of people who had lined up to shake his hand.

He was a portly man dressed in a long coat, his trademark red carnation pinned to his lapel. The president had practically been elected on his hand shaking. He could grip and squeeze fifty hands a minute and leave everyone feeling special.

Squeeze, shake, how d'ee do? They flowed past, the beautiful American people. All colors, sizes and shapes.

Behind him the organist, dwarfed by the gleaming pipes rising all the way to the ceiling, swayed and pounded.

Unseeing and unseen, the small white cat came padding toward the music. It was cascading now. Yes, it was like a waterfall, but one he wanted to be near. A waterfall of sound.

The next person in the reception line was a young crumpled-looking man with flitting blue eyes. His hand was in his pocket. Only when the president extended his hand did the young man reciprocate and draw his out.

A handkerchief was wrapped around it. He must have been injured, or perhaps maimed and ashamed, President McKinley thought just before the shots rang out.

The organ stopped. The president's face drained of blood as he blinked in incomprehension.

He took one step back, then crumpled to the ground.

After the shooting, the Pan-American Exposition closed for several days. Where before it had been wondrously illuminated by two hundred and forty thousand electric lights powered by Niagara Falls, now tragedy veiled it in darkness.

During this time Giancarlo lingered in his hiding place in the bushes. He'd heard the shots and seen the stampede of terrified spectators fleeing the Temple of Music. He'd watched the assassin led away by the police, and the president carried out on a stretcher.

When the crowd at last dispersed, Giancarlo stepped inside the empty building, trying to understand what had happened. That was when he noticed something lying near the organ. A trampled white handkerchief, he thought.

No. It was the cat. Giancarlo gathered him up — alive! Then a man in a uniform appeared and began to shout. Giancarlo fled.

What kind of place was this America, he had to wonder now. To a frightened, hungry boy, it seemed hard and cruel.

Pudding was feeling something similar. The day he walked out of the barn, he'd been so eager to experience the wide world. He'd survived a plunge down Niagara Falls and a dunking in the river. And now he'd been trampled by a stampeding crowd. He could still hear the deafening shots and smell their bitter, powdery odor.

But worst of all was the sight of the old lion in the cage. All the animals — unfree. The opposite of adventuring.

Mother Tat had tried to warn him that the wide world was a dangerous place. "Be careful," she used to whisper to him.

Now he believed her.

The trampling left him with a gash on his back that he couldn't reach to wash and a rear leg too sore to bear weight. Giancarlo nursed him as best he could. He scavenged scraps to eat from the now quiet train station, fair food discarded in a rush when the exposition closed. Half-eaten frankfurters, whole peanuts among the discarded shells.

Though he was hungry himself, he sucked on a sandwich crust to soften it and offered it to the injured cat.

"A crust now?" the flea said with disgust. "I want roast beef. I want it in bed. A soft bed. I want a view out the window. And carpets. Electric lights, too."

He crossed two legs over his hard brown chest and stamped the other four.

"I can't walk," Pudding said.

The flea heaved a sigh. "I really should have picked the tabby."

In the mildest of tones, Pudding replied, "Hop off if you like."

"Hop off?" the flea screamed. "What do you mean? You're my *host*. You're responsible for my health and happiness!"

What a patient and kind-hearted cat Pudding was! Only now did he do what you or I would have done ages ago.

He stuck his unhurt rear paw in his ear and scratched.

"Ahhhh!!!!"

The surprised parasite went flying through the air and landed a yard away. He picked himself up, brushed himself off with four of his six legs and bounded right back.

"What did you do that for?"

"I thought you wanted another host."

"Do you see another cat around here? Believe me, as soon as one shows up, I'm hopping off this bus."

He was so mad that he squatted in Pudding's ear and refused to speak.

Bliss.

4
+ NEW YORK CITY +
1901

The day the Exposition reopened, Giancarlo woke cold and sore. Now he would have to stand at the gate grinding the organ again. Like before, no one would even look at a filthy, monkeyless boy.

The monkey! He burst into sobs. He would never earn enough to pay for the monkey and get back to New York, let alone home to Laurenzana.

Then he looked at the white creature in his arms. The cat was lucky. Lucky and gentle, too. Unlike the monkey.

He stopped crying. The clothes! The cat was almost the same size as the monkey.

"I can't see a thing!" the flea complained as Giancarlo tied the bonnet strings under Pudding's chin.

Pudding didn't mind the hat, for its broad brim shielded his eyes. It was the dress he didn't care for.

The cat under one arm, Giancarlo dragged the barrel organ out from under the bush and closer to the gate. He set Pudding on it and held him there by the collar.

"Who turned out the lights?" the flea hollered.

"What's going on?

Now, for the first time in this new country, Giancarlo sang. He turned the crank on the organ and threw back his head. The trip across the ocean, his failure as an organ grinder, how he'd stood in line to meet the president only to see him shot.

He belted out his whole sad story.

"Listen to him blubber," the flea said in disgust.

More and more people stopped to listen. Some were moved by the boy's beautiful voice and the suffering they heard there, some by the sight of a child alone and obviously faring badly. So dirty! Holes bigger than his shoes!

Some were delighted by the frocked cat who sat atop the organ, eyes closed and bonnet tilted, listening so intently.

Their hearts opened and so did their purses.

Soon Giancarlo realized that he didn't need to hold onto Pudding. All the better to receive the pennies that fell into his open palm.

Three hours later he was on the train bound for New York with Pudding in the carpet bag in his lap. He'd bought a fresh roll in the station to share with the cat, but it did little to quiet the grumbling in his belly.

"In Laurenzana," he told Pudding, "we're poor, but we always have enough to eat. On feast days they move the long tables into the square and pile the platters high. Sausages and calzone, gnocchi with turnip. Pastries. *Gatto,* I'm going home and I'm going to take you with me."

He made this promise to the cat knowing in his heart and in his noisy stomach that he would be serving three years in America the way his father had.

Inside the dark carpet bag Pudding drowsed, still savoring the boy's singing. Yes, the wide world could be cruel. It was full of peril. He understood this now. But there was music in it!

"From barrel to bush to bag," the flea said. "Cripes!"

The train screeched into Grand Central Station and Giancarlo clumsily disembarked with the organ and the cat-filled bag. He began his long, burdened trudge back to the tenement on Crosby Street, filled with dread as each step took him closer to the padrone.

At the same time Giancarlo was struggling along, Vincent Bryan was traveling down Third Avenue toward him in the most astonishing contraption. An "automobile." It looked like a regular carriage, but somehow it moved "auto" — on its own. Without a horse! Instead of reins, you steered it with a rod mounted with a shiny brass horn.

Vincent had seen a few automobiles on the road,

but he never imagined that one day he would ride in one. Yet this was what his crazy friend Gus Edwards had shown up in. He called it an Oldsmobile.

As if driving such a thing didn't attract enough attention, Gus kept honking the horn. It made an odd *blat-blat* sound that spooked the horse trotting alongside them.

As the animal surged ahead, the driver shouted over his shoulder at Gus, "Get that newfangled menace off the road!"

Vincent shrank down in the seat, but Gus just laughed.

They passed a knickerbockered newsboy on the corner with his stack of papers under his arm. For a whole block the boy ran beside them, calling, "Gimme a ride, eh, mister? Would you? Pretty please!"

A young lady in a plumed hat stopped to watch them pass. Gus honked at her, too.

What a guy! Gus was only a year older than Vincent, twenty-two, but he had three times the confidence. He'd grown up in New York and had been singing in saloons and clubs since he was a kid. A natty dresser, too. He oiled his black hair until it gleamed. Putt-putting the autumn streets of Manhattan, the subject of astonished stares and delighted gapes, flirting with women. That was Gus.

Vincent had arrived the year before from that

far-off pile of rocks, Newfoundland. He, too, was on the move. One of the dreamers, dreaming big of a vaudeville career. But so far it hadn't happened. He couldn't even get the look right. He couldn't afford the high shirt collars Gus wore. And, no matter how much hair oil Vincent applied, his curls wouldn't lie down.

"You're going to see more of these," Gus said. He squeezed the horn — *blat!* "The streets are going to be full of them."

"Automobiles?" Vincent said. "I can't see it. I mean, what do you feed it?"

"Gasoline."

A dog darted across the road.

"Watch it," Vincent said, and Gus jerked the steering rod. They swerved down a street near Union Square, half torn up for the new subway. A long trench ran the whole length of the block. Vincent could see the workers deep inside sledgehammering and shoveling.

Gus pointed to the trench. "Nobody believed in the subway either. By the way, I have a title for our song."

"We're writing a song?" Vincent asked.

"'In My Merry Oldsmobile.' What do you think?"

"A song about driving?"

"A song that everybody'll be singing when they

get themselves one of these." *Blat-blat!* "We'll make a fortune! I've even got a bit of the tune." He whistled it.

Vincent looked around for inspiration. A streetcar ahead. Horse and cart congestion. Subway workers tipping rubble into a cart. As they turned to stare, the whites of their astonished eyes glowed in their dirt-blackened faces. It was miserable work. How long before Vincent would be working alongside them?

He closed his eyes and imagined someone besides him in the Oldsmobile. Not a nervous newcomer from Newfoundland worried about his future, but a bold young man called …

"*Young Johnny has an Oldsmobile,*" Vincent sang to Gus's tune.

"Vincie! You *are* good! I could tell when I heard you playing at the Black Cat."

Just as Gus said this, a real boy came into view. He was the ragged kind Vincent saw everywhere in New York. This one was lugging a carpet bag in one hand and dragging a wooden box. How could someone so small carry so much?

As they got closer, he saw the strap around his neck. A barrel organ.

"Watch out!" Vincent yelled.

The Oldsmobile sideswiped the boy and sent him

toppling into the gutter. Gus braked. He and Vincent jumped out and joined the concerned passersby gathering around the boy. He seemed unhurt, but he was hysterical over the bag.

"What's he got in there?" someone asked.

"*Gatto, gatto,*" the boy wailed, clutching the bag.

A stout woman in a kerchief pried away his fingers. They got the briefest glimpse inside before the boy snatched the bag back.

Stained white fur.

Gus groaned. "I killed his cat." He took off his hat. "I'm sorry about your *gatto*, kid. Honest."

"It would've been the kid if he wasn't carrying the bag!" said a brawny unshaven man in shirtsleeves. He towered over Gus.

Gus tapped the crying boy's shoulder and pointed to the Oldsmobile in the middle of the road. Then he nodded to Vincent, who took the organ and slung it on the platform behind the seat. The stout woman nudged the boy.

At last he picked himself up and followed, sniffing and smearing tears and snot around his face, leaving muddy streaks. He seemed afraid to get into the automobile.

Gus gave him a boost. When they were all seated, he asked, "Where to?"

The boy pointed straight ahead. As soon as they

began to move, his face bloomed with wonderment. He peered at the steering rod, then down at the pedals Gus was working with his feet. Reaching out a filthy hand, he touched the dashboard. Every time they turned a corner, he smiled. Then he would look down at the bag in his lap and well up again with tears.

Down to the Lower East Side they drove, to the dark rows of tenements, the grimy shops with their soiled awnings, the tattery sails of laundry flying from the fire escapes. The boy seemed oblivious to the stares of the people they passed — untamed children like him, a ragged peddler, his cart clinking with pots.

Finally, he gestured to a building fronted by a pair of smoking ash cans. Gus stopped, and Vincent stepped down onto the cobbles to let the boy out.

"Take the bag," Gus told Vincent. "We'll throw it in the river for him."

When Vincent reached for the carpet bag, the boy renewed his wails. Gus jumped out and opened his wallet. What he offered was more than the boy had ever seen in his life. Vincent knew this because it was more than *he* had ever seen.

The boy glanced at the building and, shuddering, took the money. Off he staggered, dragging the organ and bawling like an opera singer.

And what about poor Pudding Tat?

Don't worry. When the Oldsmobile passed Giancarlo, the engine crank snagged the carpet bag and sent him spinning. The stain they'd glimpsed when the bag was opened was from his trampling in the Temple of Music, the gash on his back he'd been unable to reach with his tongue.

"Now what's happening?" the flea harrumphed.

The unfamiliar *put-putting* of the Oldsmobile caught Pudding's curious ear. The sounds of the city, too — carriage wheels on cobbles, clopping hooves, the singsong cries of newsboys. The clanking and grating of the work crews.

Eventually, he meowed.

When Vincent heard the cat, he thought he was imagining it. He reached over the seat for the bag and opened it in his lap.

There was Pudding, calicoed with dried blood, squirming in the light.

"He's alive!" Vincent cried.

Blat-blat! Blat-blat! Blat-blat! Gus honked.

Vincent noticed the cat's closed eyes and how he kept burying his head to get away from the light. He closed the bag again and didn't open it until they were in his Greenwich Village apartment with the curtains drawn.

Now Pudding peeped out at a pleasantly dim room. He lifted his nose and sniffed.

Mice!

"What a dump!" the flea exclaimed.

Pudding crawled out of the bag and settled down for a wash just as Gus sat at Vincent's piano and began tinkling out the tune he'd whistled earlier.

An ecstatic shiver ran through Pudding. He limped toward the piano.

Vincent scooped him up and set him on top. Then they got down to business, Gus on the music, Vincent spinning out the lyrics, both of them singing snatches.

Come away with me, Lucille,
in my merry Oldsmobile!
Down the road of life we'll fly,
automobubbling, you and I!

Pudding perched there with his eyes closed and his white tail tucked around his feet, not just hearing the music but feeling it beneath him.

After an hour, Gus stood to stretch. As soon as the music stopped, Pudding leapt three-footedly down onto the keyboard. The sound of the notes smashing together so surprised him that he froze and listened until the vibrations died away.

Vincent and Gus watched to see what he would do next. Pudding reached out a paw and poked. A pure note sounded.

"He's purring," Vincent said.

When that note faded, Pudding poked out another.

"That's it!" Gus cried.

He sat down again at the piano and, reaching between and around the cat's white feet, he tinkled out the next bar.

That night the flea said a surprising thing. "You're blind."

"Hold on," Pudding told him. He was hoping to land his first New York meal. A whole extended family of mice lived in the walls. One had come out to forage. Pudding could see its meaty back as it gathered up crumbs. He limped painfully toward it.

It had been a long time since he'd tasted mouse. He couldn't wait.

"I can't believe I only just figured it out! That's why you crash into things. Why you let yourself get picked up and stuffed into barrels and bags."

Pudding lost his concentration. "During the day …" he started to explain.

The mouse looked up and, seeing a pink pair of blinking eyes, scrammed.

"... I prefer to keep my eyes closed."

Pudding wasn't worried about losing the mouse. Moments later another emerged from the hole in the baseboard and replaced the relative who'd taken fright. Pudding crouched and prepared to stalk his prey. Finally he was a hunter again, one of the Great Race of Tats, the Fearless Pudding the First!

"Boy, did I pick wrong!" the flea said. "Boy-o-boy! No wonder you've dragged me through so much trouble. And for what? This place? Maybe you can't see it, but I can. Broken-down furniture. Stained rug. He calls those curtains? Rags!"

He kicked the wall of Pudding's ear, making it twitch.

"There's no way I'm staying here!"

But to his host — a music-loving, mouse-eating cat — a pianoed apartment in the vermin-teeming city of New York seemed the perfect resting place.

Word soon got around about Vincent Bryan and his amazing composing cat.

"Pure white and blind," Gus Edwards told everybody. "Sits on top of the piano. Every now and then he jumps down on the keyboard and makes a suggestion."

Gus exaggerated, everyone knew that. But now

when Vincent played, people knew who he was. "The guy from Newfoundland with the composing cat, right?"

By the time Pudding's leg and back had healed, Vincent was writing extra music and lyrics for a play called *The Wizard of Oz*.

In the evenings, while Vincent was playing at the Black Cat, Pudding sat on the windowsill waiting for the late-night crowd to spill out of the clubs. Musicians, painters and poets — they were a parade of shadows to him. All young with artistic hair and bright clothes, they expressed themselves in new ways, in ragtime and jazz. They danced in bare feet, painted in smears and wrote poems that didn't rhyme.

They were changing the stodgy old wide world.

When the streets filled like this, Pudding knew to expect that familiar tune, the one Vincent always whistled on his way home. Though it was three o'clock in the morning and he was tired, Vincent would always sit at the piano and play one last song for his beloved cat.

The next morning, hungering for music again, Pudding would stroll across the piano keys. If that didn't wake Vincent up, he'd jump on the bed and knead his pajamaed chest. While Vincent oiled his hair, Pudding would weave impatiently around his legs.

At last, Vincent sat at the piano, and the complaints streaming from the flea were drowned out once again.

What did the flea complain about? The same old things! This place was beneath him.

"It stinks. This is the kind of dump those drunken poo-eaters would feel at home in. The only decent place you brought me to was that hotel. I want a bed like that again."

"There's a bed here."

"I want one with an old lady in it to feed you things I like. I deserve it."

"What have you done to deserve it?" Pudding asked.

"I don't have to *do* anything. *Doing* is what the host is for. I just *am*. Take me away."

In truth, although Pudding still wanted to reach the four corners of the wide world, he was worried about what would happen to him when he left. Until something piqued his curiosity, he'd stay put.

Before long, something did.

They'd been living in Greenwich Village for several months when it happened.

First, everything grew very quiet. Then a strange soft light began to fill the small apartment. Outside, people started to laugh and call to each other, but their voices seemed muffled.

What was going on?

Pudding leapt onto the windowsill and looked out. Greenwich Village was fast disappearing behind a curtain of white.

That night, back on his windowsill perch, Pudding waited for Vincent's whistling.

"*Come away with me, Lucille ...*"

He leapt down from the sill and went over to the door.

"Are we really going?" the astonished flea asked.

Pudding heard the door to the building open. Vincent came whistling up the two flights of stairs. The moment he stepped inside, Pudding slipped out between his feet and dashed down the hall, hugging the wall.

A white cat is easy to see in the dark. Vincent noticed Pudding's escape but went first to set his satchel of music on the table. He didn't believe the cat could get any farther than the vestibule downstairs.

He was just coming down the second flight of stairs when another night owl came in the front door of the building.

"Don't let the cat out!" Vincent yelled.

Too late.

Open-eyed Pudding ran along the snowy street. Only when he'd turned a corner did he pause to marvel at what was beneath his feet. He lifted each paw, set it down again. Such a delicate squeak it made, this cold, cat-concealing cover that had fallen over the village.

"Giddy-up," the flea said. "Find me a classy cat, not some mouse-eater. Maybe a Persian."

Such a beautiful hush as the feathery flakes fell. Pudding padded on. In the distance, the familiar night sounds were muted. The gurgling of the ice-making factory, the rumble of the Sixth Avenue elevated train.

Then, as he passed under the triumphal arch in Washington Square, he heard a yowl.

"Cat!" cried the flea.

It was a tomcat summoning one of his wives, his cry a deep, slow ululation.

As Pudding drew nearer to the snow-covered bench where the tomcat sang, he saw an intimidating silhouette, enormous and thick-necked.

The tomcat saw Pudding, too, and rose slowly from his crouch. His back arched and his tail swelled.

"I don't like the look of that one," the flea said.

Under his wailing song, a hundred voices belted out. They were the tomcat's fleas, stamping their legion feet and tunelessly chanting.

Get that cat!
Squirt its blood!

Drink it up!
Fee fi fo yum!

It made "The Bloodless Flea's Lament" sound like a nursery rhyme.

Pudding began to back away.

The flea wailed, "He's going to kill you! Run!"

Just then Vincent appeared out of the whiteness. He'd been following Pudding's paw prints in the snow. Relieved, he scooped him up.

"Don't run away," he cooed. "We have a lot more songs to write."

After their outing, the flea went right back to complaining. To relieve his own boredom, he added a few new gripes. His armored plates had lost their luster. His mouthparts no longer curled.

"It's because of all that mousy blood I'm forced to drink."

These new complaints replaced the one he never made again. He never asked for a different host.

The following spring, their situation changed. Royalties started to pour in from "In My Merry Oldsmobile," making Vincent and Gus rich. Soon after, the flea's wish came true. Vincent, Pudding and his flea moved uptown.

The new building had an elevator. There was a doorman, too, who touched the brim of his cap and greeted Vincent with, "Ev'ning, Mr. Bryan."

A huge apartment with plush carpets, plump cushions and velvet drapes.

"Oooh-la-la!" the flea shrieked when they were set down in the middle of it.

Pudding lifted his nose in the air and sniffed.

Nothing.

Vincent toured with an orchestra now. While he was away, which was often, the doorman came to feed Pudding his dinner of minced steak doused with cream.

"Ev'ning, Mr. Bryan's cat," he'd say.

Sometimes, if the doorman dared leave his post long enough, he'd put a record on the gramophone.

"Listen to this, Mr. Bryan's cat. Mr. Bryan wrote this song. It says so right here on the sleeve. He's famous."

"Come away with me, Lucille, in my merry Oldsmobile ..."

This was about the only time Pudding heard music now.

So began the untraveled part of Pudding Tat's much-traveled life. The boring part. There was little for an adventurous cat to do in that posh, mouseless apartment where the piano was left shut to keep the dust off the keyboard.

Not that there was any dust. A maid came to clean every week. Pudding's windowsill perch was now nine stories up — too high for him to see anything interesting in the street. The closed window sealed out most smells and sounds.

In the beginning Pudding tried to imagine that he was still a mighty hunter of the Great Race of Tats. He crept soundlessly over the carpets and pounced on figments. Or he stuck his foot in his ear, scratched, and sent the flea flying, then ran off and hid under the divan, pretending that the flea was hunting *him*.

The flea bounded frantically from room to room. "Yoo-hoo? Where are you, you tasty rascal! Come out, come out, wherever you are!"

When the flea finally found Pudding, he jabbed his mouthparts in deep again. "Yum. Tasty. Dee-lish." He belched. "Remember back in that horrible barn? The stinky horses and cows? All those disgusting fleas with their songs? Back then I took one look at you and said, 'There's the host for me.' Yes, I've been through tough times. But look at me now. Look!" He'd swelled out to the point of popping his armored plates. "This is what I was born for!"

Pudding did have some glorious washes during those years. Morning and evening, with touch-ups throughout the day. He spent hours running his tongue over every white inch of himself. Then he would cough up the by-product. A hairball to relieve his tedium.

Here is a summary of his daily activities. Sleep, sleep, sleep, sleep, sleep. Wash. Sleep, sleep. Eat. Wash. Sleep, sleep, sleep, sleep. Wash. Sleep, sleep, sleep. Wash.

Under these conditions Pudding's longings shriveled, even his longing for music. He grew sleepy and fat. The sleepier he felt, the more he slept. In his dreams he was still a svelte white cat catching mice in Vincent's Greenwich Village apartment, flinging them in the air to give them a chance before his decisive pounce. Or he was back in the barn with his brothers and sisters, stalking dinner together.

As for his actual adventures — the plunge down Niagara Falls, his escape from the barrel, the President's assassination — he thought he'd dreamed them, too.

Then one day, Pudding woke to the sound of singing.

"Oh, the flea jumped on the dog!"

He could hardly believe his sleepy ears. Had that gang of drunken fleas returned?

No. Instead of a chorus, a lone voice warbled.

From cat to dog,
From dog to horse,
From horse to cow,
He drank their blood, hey ho!

"Is that really you?" Pudding asked.

"Who?" the flea slurred.

He paused to kick out his legs in clumsy dance. Then he went right back to glugging Pudding's blood.

5
+ ATLANTIC CITY, NEW JERSEY +
1910

Had the flea realized he'd escaped the barn only to end up living the life he'd fled, he would have been horrified.

But he didn't. Like his five hundred and ninety-nine brothers and sisters and all the *Ctenocephalides felis* before him, he was too busy drinking blood and belting out drunken ditties.

When the flea sang — if we can call it that — Pudding remembered the joyful purr-mew-nicker-clank of his kittenhood in the barn with his brothers and sisters and dear Mother Tat. He remembered the buzz-huff-hum-twitter-thrum-scratch-squeak and the rustle-sigh of the wind. Sounds he never heard now, except in his dreams.

Meanwhile, the wide world kept on changing. People were moving around even more, and in new ways. The subway stretched the length of Manhattan, all the way to the Bronx. There were automobiles everywhere.

And since the Wright brothers first lifted into the air in 1903, that amazing invention, the aeroplane, was breaking new records.

In the summer of 1910, Vincent Bryan and Gus Edwards booked a week in the Chalfonte Hotel in Atlantic City. They went for the Air Carnival. Flying teams competed for prizes while below them, huge crowds lined the boardwalk and beaches waving pennants and swooning from excitement and heat stroke.

Air travel was the big dream now. The famous explorer Walter Wellman was in Atlantic City, too, but with a much different machine: an airship. A few years before, Mr. Wellman had attempted to reach the North Pole. Now he hoped to be the first to cross the Atlantic Ocean by air.

It turned out that Mr. Wellman and his crew were also staying in the Chalfonte Hotel. At breakfast, friendly Gus chatted up their Australian wireless man, Jack Irwin, who was about their age. By the end of the meal he'd invited them to visit the balloon house on the outskirts of Atlantic City.

The next day they found themselves in an enormous canvas hangar, staring up at the airship. It looked like a gigantic floating cigar.

"Fancy taking a ride in that," Vincent said.

"It's how we'll all be traveling in a few years," Gus said. "How about we write another song, Vincie? 'In My Merry Airship.'"

"I just can't see it," Vincent said, scratching his head.

"I can't either, to tell you the truth," Jack told

them. "I've crossed the Atlantic more times than I can count. By sea. Rather do it on an ocean liner."

"Why?"

"It's safer." He looked away, tugging on the knot of his tie as though it was too tight.

"Even with icebergs and whatnot?" Gus reached into his pocket and took out his cigarette case.

A horrified look crossed the wireless man's face. "You can't smoke in here, mate. That balloon's filled with hydrogen gas. Do you want to blow us up?"

After they got back to the hotel, Vincent and Gus took in Atlantic City's other amusements. They met up with a couple of girls to ride the Loop the Loop on Young's Pier. They swam in their knitted bathing costumes and ate enough saltwater taffy to make themselves seasick. At the end of the day they strolled the crowded boardwalk, admiring the famous sand sculptures. A president, a sleeping elephant, a cobra rearing from its pile of coils — all life-sized.

Gus pointed. "And there's our merry Oldsmobile."

An Oldsmobile made of sand! The girls ran off to find a photographer. Gus and Vincent jumped down onto the beach and posed with it.

Not far from where Mr. Wellman and his crew were preparing to fly across the Atlantic Ocean, the former adventurer Pudding Tat crouched in the darkness under a hotel room bed. Vincent, feeling guilty about leaving the cat on his own so much, had decided to bring him along.

By day, while the bright summer sun sparked off the ocean, under the bed was where Pudding stayed. So many intriguing sounds and smells! The hollow roar of the ocean. Calliope music from the amusement piers. Salt breezes and fried clams and gasoline.

At the end of the day, Vincent returned to wash and dress for the evening, bringing with him a newspaper package of treats for the cat. Fat Pudding emerged and climbed into Vincent's lap. Vincent stroked his beautiful white fur until it crackled with electricity.

The flea, meanwhile, was booming out "The Bloodless Flea's Lament." He'd said nothing about the luxurious Chalfonte Hotel. He didn't even realize they'd left New York.

One day, as the maid was stripping the bed above him, Pudding peeked out. Through watering eyes he saw her stuff the sheets into the wicker hamper in the bottom of her trolley.

The maid didn't notice a white cat in the basket of white sheets until she reached the hotel basement where they sorted the soiled linen. She tipped the hamper onto the floor. Out of the pile shot something white. It streaked across the room. She screamed, and Pudding dashed out the back of the hotel.

Under the glaring eye of the sun, he hurried from shadow to shadow. The flea stopped singing when he realized an escape was in progress.

"What are you doing? Go back! Watch out! That's the —"

Pudding heard the honk of an automobile, a screech.

"Turn! Turn!"

The flea guided his host to safety under the long boardwalk.

The sound of thousands of tramping feet and laughing voices fell through the wooden slats with the melted ice cream and spilled beer. After so long indoors, the odors and noise — not to mention the strong light — overwhelmed Pudding. He waited for night to fall.

Night was quieter, except for the flea, who really had something to complain about now. Pudding hadn't eaten since the day before. His fatty blood was thinning.

"I feel sick," the flea wailed. "Take me back. Oh, my aching head! *No sadder flea!* My throat is parched! *No sadder flea he, than a bloodless* ... I'm dying!"

The beaches had emptied and there was no one to see a white cat traveling across the white sand. Pudding disliked the feeling of it between his toes, accustomed as he was now to walking on carpets. With each crash of the waves, he cringed.

Water! How he hated it!

"It's been a long time," he told the flea. "Maybe we don't belong out here anymore."

He was losing his nerve. When he paused to shake out his paws, he noticed something just ahead watching him.

He blinked. Not because his eyes hurt, but because he could not believe them.

A lion?

The only other lion he'd seen was in Bostock's Zoological Arena. Pudding had fled at the sight of him, dejected in his prison.

He drew closer to the creature, circled it one, two, three times.

It was made of sand.

He could be a free cat or a captive one, Pudding realized. A real cat or a pretend one.

"I think I'll keep going," he said.

For two days Pudding trudged through a windy expanse of dunes, surviving on fish carcasses and sea grass. By day the sun tormented him. Day and night thirst did. He was already thinner, his beautiful fur clumped by salt spray.

The flea's singing grew less raucous. Eventually it petered out like a tuneless music box winding down. Several hours of moaning followed, then a whole day of silence.

Then out of the blue a sober voice spoke. "Uggh! This is the worst blood I've ever tasted."

"Hello," Pudding said. "Are you back?"

"From where?"

"Up until now you've been hey-ho-ing and telling jokes."

"I wasn't!"

"How do you find where a flea has bitten you?" Pudding asked. *"You start from scratch."*

The flea had a conniption.

"I would never!" he shrieked. "I've got class! I'm better than them!" His voice turned croaky and hoarse. "You're lying!"

In his rage, he leapt right out of Pudding's ear and landed several feet away, sobbing. A long bout of snuffling followed. Then a quavering question.

"Was I really singing?"

Pudding stepped carefully over to where the voice had come from. Even if his eyes had been open it would have been impossible to see the miserable flea crouching among the grains of sand.

"Are you okay?" Pudding asked.

"Get lost!"

Pudding didn't. The flea might try to jump back on.

He didn't want to stray too far so he curled up in a clump of scrubby bushes. He was terribly thirsty. Hungry, too. Though he heard mice scurrying through the dunes, he couldn't catch them.

A few hours later, he felt a tickle in his ear. It was the flea crawling back. Without a word, Pudding rose and began to walk.

Just before dawn, he chanced upon a rabbit carcass, pounced on it and began to pull hungrily at the left-behind shreds of flesh.

The flea broke his silence. "Who do you think killed that rabbit?"

Pudding looked around. "Who?"

"A fox, I'm guessing," the flea said. "'Be careful.' Wasn't that what your mother said?"

"I'm a Tat," Pudding said. "Strong and brave."

"Yeah, yeah," the flea said. "Listen. I know I'm just a speck in your ear. A good-for-nothing *Ctenocephalides felis*. But if you'll permit me an opinion, this isn't the best place to hang around."

Pudding couldn't believe how modest his vain parasite sounded.

"Are you *my* flea?" he asked.

"I'd be honored if you thought of me that way," the flea said. Then he meekly suggested, "How about we skedaddle?"

Pudding left the carcass and began to trudge on, his head lowered against the wind and blowing sand.

After a few minutes the flea spoke again. "Why did you wait?"

"Pardon?" Pudding said.

"Back there. You could have kept walking and left me."

"There wasn't any other *Felis domesticus* around. You wouldn't have a host."

"Felis domesticus?" the flea asked. "That's you?"

"Yes."

"So we're *Felis* and *felis*?"

Though Pudding couldn't see it, the flea wiped his mouthparts and smiled. Then he said, "Well, if we don't clear out of these sand hills fast, we two *felises* will be lunch."

Pudding crossed the windy crest. Beyond was a road, which he began to follow. He smelled water.

"There's a bridge," the flea told him. "And a huge tent."

Pudding carried on toward it. He was on the verge of perishing of thirst.

The huge tent was Mr. Wellman's canvas balloon house, glowing from the inside. The crew was still at work.

Just then the wireless man, Jack Irwin, set the gramophone needle on the record.

"Down the road of life we'll fly," he sang. *"Aero-mobubbling you and I!"*

He heard meowing behind him and turned.

A cat!

"Why, *dah dah di, di*! Good evening! Where did you come from, Kiddo?" Jack asked. He scooped up the feline visitor. A stray, obviously, with a matted coat and closed eyes.

Jack took the cat around, introducing him to the others at work around the airship.

"Mr. Wellman? Look who dropped in for a visit."

Mr. Wellman was hunched behind a typewriter, peering through his spectacles, writing his latest bulletin on the progress of their expedition. He barely glanced up.

"He's the man in charge, Kiddo."

Jack carried him over to the first engineer, who was tinkering with the motors. "And here we have Mr. Vaniman. Don't let him touch you with those greasy hands."

"I hate cats!" Mr. Vaniman cried, waving Jack away. His hands weren't only dirty, but enormous. "Get him out of here!"

"Hey, Vaniman," said the navigator, Mr. Simon, who wore his straw boater hat day and night. He was neat and fussy where Mr. Vaniman was burly and rough. "Be nice. A cat on a ship is good luck."

"Even a cat on an airship?" Mr. Vaniman scoffed.

"Why not? A ship is a ship."

"Stick around and you'll see a bit of history, Kiddo," Jack whispered to the cat. Then he noticed that the creature's eyes were still closed. "I guess you won't."

Jack fashioned a bed out of some of some spare silk left over from the balloon. He got the cat a bowl of water and opened a tin of sardines. Pudding drank and drank. Once his terrible thirst was slaked, he gobbled the food and licked the tin clean.

Meanwhile, Jack wound the gramophone again and lowered the needle on another record.

"Oh! ... that beautiful rag! It sets my heart a-reelin' ..."

Ragtime filling his ears, Pudding curled up in the silk bed and fell into an exhausted sleep.

Sometime near morning, the flea spoke. "What is *that*?"

Pudding woke. He could just make out in the vast space of the balloon house an enormous long shadow above them.

Curious, he walked all the way around the airship until he found an opening in the cloth-covered passenger car underneath. He clawed his way up the canvas and slipped inside, inspecting the benches, the steering wheel, the navigation equipment.

Adventure. His tingling whiskers sensed it.

Jack Irwin had come from Australia to train as a sea-going wireless operator with the Marconi Wireless Telegraph Company of America. What a life, traveling back and forth across the Atlantic Ocean, clicking out the *di*s and *dah*s of Morse Code.

Then last spring his boss called him to the company office and asked if he wanted to be part of the Wellman expedition.

"It'll be the first crossing of the Atlantic Ocean by air. Mr. Wellman needs a wireless for weather reports and to send dispatches to the newspapers. The whole world will be following. Interested?"

Dah di dah dah, di, di di di, Jack thought before blurting it out. "Yes!"

It was only after the word left his mouth that he remembered the hydrogen gas. The wireless machine sent its *di*s and *dah*s through electric sparks. If a spark from the wireless machine somehow escaped …

Jack had nightmares about the airship exploding. His nerves only settled when he arrived at the balloon house and was greeted by the little white cat who had mysteriously appeared one night. Just the sight of him eased his fears.

"Dah dah di, dah dah!" Good morning!

As the cat rubbed against his legs, Jack couldn't help but hear a code in the animal's purring.

"Take me with you," he seemed to be saying. *"Di dah dah di, di di di, di." Please.*

When visitors dropped in, everyone wanted to see the little cat who was going to make history with them.

"No, he's not," insisted the youngest of Mr. Wellman's five daughters, Edith. "Daddy promised *I* could have Kitty."

"I named him Kiddo," Jack said.

"He's mine and I call him Kitty."

They were ready to launch by September, but winds delayed them again and again. Finally, in mid-October, a bang came on Jack's door in the Chalfonte Hotel.

He'd been, as usual, dreaming in Morse Code. Dreaming of clicking out those terrible letters: CQD.

Dah di dah di, dah dah di dah, dah di di. All Stations — Distress!

Then the spark met the hydrogen. *BOOM!!!*

"Irwin!" came the shout with the hammering fist. "All clear! We're leaving!"

Jack shot out of his bad dream and his bed. He leapt into trousers, which he kept nearby with the tops of his boots already inside the legs. In minutes he was dressed and running down the hotel stairs and out into a cold foggy morning.

The commotion in the balloon house woke Pudding. He knew it meant departure, for he'd heard it often with Vincent — the bustling and packing, the nervous energy. No one put on the gramophone. Jack forgot his sardines.

Pudding trailed after him, meowing at his ankles.

On the beach a massive crowd gathered — journalists, spectators and two hundred police and firemen Mr. Wellman had enlisted to launch the *America*. When the crew drew back the canvas doors, revealing the airship, everyone gave up a collective gasp.

"Would you look at the size of it!"

"Where do they sit?"

"The long bit underneath. See the windows? They fly the thing from there. The lifeboat hangs below it. That's where they keep the wireless machine."

"I can't hardly believe my eyes!"

"Could a bloodsucking nobody suggest that you step aside?" the flea piped up, just as the men came marching in.

Pudding remembered well his long-ago trampling in the Temple of Music. His left rear foot still throbbed before a storm. He dove to safety under the workbench.

"Heave-ho!" Mr. Wellman called.

The men shouldered the ropes and, inch by inch, dragged the airship out.

"Stay back!" the flea kept warning Pudding.

But he didn't want to be left behind. When the canvas fell closed again and the voices began to recede, he crawled out from under the workbench into the dim vacancy of the balloon house.

"Good luck, Mr. Wellman!" someone called.

"We'll be praying for you!"

"Too bad about the fog. We won't see it in a minute."

Then Pudding heard a needling voice. "Kitty! Here, Kitty, Kitty!"

"Oh, cripes," the flea groaned. "We don't want to get stuck with her."

Pudding slipped back under the bench, but Edith saw him and dragged him out by the scruff. Outside, Mr. Wellman was bellowing orders.

"Edith!" Mrs. Wellman called. "Come and kiss your father goodbye!"

With the crew aboard, the tugboat was ready to tow them to open water. Mr. Wellman, standing in the lifeboat, had been about to give the signal when he saw his youngest daughter coming toward him with the cat slack in her arms. He leaned out and pecked her cheek.

Edith screeched, for the limp cat suddenly came to life, leaping right out of her arms and into the lifeboat and under a pile of empty ballast bags.

At the same moment Mr. Wellman called to the men holding the ropes, "Let go!"

He climbed up to the car with the rest of the crew, leaving Jack in the lifeboat below with the wireless machine.

As the *America* rose into the air, a fluttering started deep inside Pudding.

The flea felt it, too. "Whoa! Where are we? What's happening?"

They were still attached to the tugboat chugging along the inlet, the airship floating behind it like a giant balloon on a string. Fog enveloped them and Pudding crawled out from under the bags. He sniffed the fishy air. In the cottony light he could open his eyes. Above him, the nose of the airship plowed through the white. A raucous convoy of gulls wheeled around them, appearing and disappearing in the fog.

"Oooh! I feel all funny inside," the flea warbled.

Jack was in his place at the wireless, his back to the cat. With shaking hands he put on his headphones. Before long he heard the station on Young's Pier calling. He shouted up to Mr. Wellman, "Receiving!"

"Answer," Mr. Wellman called down.

Jack's stomach turned over. Mr. Wellman stuck his head out of the car and, through his spectacles, met eyes with Jack. He was frightened, too, Jack could tell.

Jack took a breath, flipped the sending switch and positioned his finger above the key. As soon as he touched it there would be a spark.

And then?

"Irwin!" Mr. Wellman barked. "What are you waiting for?"

He couldn't bring himself to touch that key.

Something brushed against his leg. Something soft. He glanced down.

"Kiddo!"

His heart soared to see the cat. But it wasn't just his heart, he realized then. *All of him* was soaring. He, Jack Irwin, just a wireless man, was *flying!*

With one hand he lifted the purring cat and buried his face in the white fur. His finger pressed the key.

Dah!

Nothing but relief. Then he clicked out the rest of the code. *QSL: I acknowledge receipt.*

And for the purring cat, *Thanks.*

"*Dah, dah di dah, di di di*, Kiddo."

By the time the tugboat reached open water, Jack was sending and receiving messages fearlessly. The tug cast off their line. Untethered, the *America* lifted even higher in the fog, causing every stomach on board to lurch. Mr. Vaniman started the engines. The noisy propellers began to spin. The crew gave up a whoop.

"We're really flying now!"

Pudding shrank down in pain. His ears hurt from the engine din. Then, as the *America* rose even higher, a familiar ache settled in his bones.

The flea had no bones, just an exoskeleton. He was merely terrified.

"Woe to the flea!" he cried.

When Pudding's left rear foot began to throb, he knew. *Storm!*

He yowled out a warning.

"Is that the cat?" Mr. Vaniman bellowed down. "Throw him out!"

Mr. Simon stood at the airship's wheel with his straw boater tied on his head with a bootlace to keep it from blowing off in the wind. "It's bad luck to put a cat off a ship," he snapped.

"Leave him," Jack called up. "He'll settle down."

But Pudding only grew more frantic as the heavy air closed around him and squeezed. *Storm! Storm! Storm!* He began to tear around the lifeboat, screeching.

Finally, Mr. Vaniman had had enough. "Is he going to keep up that racket for the whole crossing? Permission to put him off? We'll drop him on the tug."

Mr. Vaniman jumped into the lifeboat. Before Pudding knew what was happening, a monstrous hand came down on him. Mr. Vaniman stuffed him into one of the canvas bags and tied the mouth with one of the ropes coiled on the floor.

The drowning sack!

Pudding screeched even louder.

"Wire the tug," Mr. Vaniman yelled to Jack. "Tell them to come and get this idiot cat!"

Jack did what he asked. He was afraid Vaniman would toss the cat overboard otherwise.

The tugboat had just turned back toward shore when it received Jack's message to come and get a stowaway cat. With the fog and the sea roiling with waves, Mr. Vaniman had trouble seeing anything. He lowered the convulsing sack anyway.

In the wind, the bag swung like a pendulum with Pudding and the flea inside it.

Water! The smell grew stronger. Pudding remembered his terrifying descent in the barrel. He thrashed and thrashed. The airship was rising, but he was going down.

Down,

down,

down,

down.

Icy water poured into his nostrils and mouth and ears, silencing him.

"No!" the flea screamed.

When the rope slackened, Mr. Vaniman assumed that the bag had landed on the deck of the tug. He waited for the signal to raise the rope again — one sharp pull. Instead, a message came in on the wireless that the tug was returning to shore. The sea was too rough.

No cat, Jack heard in the *di*s and *dah*s.

He tore off his headset and leapt at Mr. Vaniman, snatching the rope from him and hauling until the dripping bag was back on board. He lifted out the sodden cat, dunked like a teabag in the icy Atlantic.

Mr. Simon, who had sailed many ships in his time, believed that maritime traditions should be respected. He exploded when he saw the cat.

"This voyage is doomed!" he yelled at Mr. Vaniman. "Bad enough to put a cat off a ship, but to drown it like an unwanted kitten?"

Mr. Vaniman yelled back that Simon was an idiot. Mr. Wellman yelled at them both to get to their stations.

They all disappeared inside the car above, leaving Jack in the lifeboat. Gently, he lifted the body onto a dry bag, wrapped it and held it to his chest.

As when they'd swirled in the currents of the Niagara River, the flea had held on.

Now he told his host, "Buddy, can you hear me? It's your flea. *Ctenocephalides felis*."

He tugged on Pudding's ear hairs. When this had no effect, he crawled out and stood on the end of Pudding's pink nose.

"Noooooo!!!" He cried, screamed, stomped. When this had no effect, he crawled right up Pudding's nose and had his conniption in there, falling onto his back and kicking all six of his legs at once.

"This is my host! I can't live without him! I don't *want* to live without him! Take us both away!"

His tiny legs flailed and his armored plates bristled.

And Pudding sneezed. The seawater gushed right out of him, sluicing the surprised flea into the bottom of the boat.

"Kiddo!" Jack cried, overjoyed, just as the wireless began *di dah*ing. He set Pudding down and rushed to his station.

The flea crawled out of the puddle of seawater and hopped back to his host.

"Did you see what I did?" he crowed with pride. "I saved you!"

"Thank you," Pudding said, shaking himself.

"Not bad for puny bloodsucker, eh?"

He sounded like his old gloating self again. Pudding was happy to hear it.

Jack finished tapping out a reply to the incoming message. *QSL: I acknowledge receipt.* He shouted the message up to Mr. Wellman. "Gale approaching!"

"That's what the cat was trying to tell us," Mr. Simon roared back. "He's more reliable than our barometer!"

The gale Pudding predicted blew the airship off course the second day. The wind battered them, but they lashed tight the canvas and adjusted their altitude. Mr. Simon's straw boater tore off his head, but that was the worst of the damage.

After the gale, calm descended and for several hours they sailed smoothly. Pudding was welcomed in the airship proper, where Mr. Simon lifted him onto his shoulder while he steered. With the breeze ruffling his white fur, he truly felt like an adventuring cat. In his ear, the self-satisfied flea sang a rousing chorus of "Oh, I'm a Jolly Good Flea."

But soon Pudding's sensitive ears picked out a new sound, a sputtering that, when it grew loud enough for human hearing, brought Mr. Vaniman racing to the engines. He tried to repair the ailing one, but it shuddered and died. It took the whole crew to heave it overboard.

By the third day, already far off course due to the storm and the altered weight of the ship, Pudding felt that ache again in his left foot. He set off his warning and this time everyone paid attention, even before the wireless message came in.

A hurricane was heading their way this time. With just one engine, they would never survive it.

Four hundred miles off the coast, Jack sent the message he'd delivered so often in his nightmares: *CQD: All Stations — Distress!*

Luckily, a Royal Mail ship from England happened along. It picked up the crew and their cat. The *America*, abandoned, was snatched up by the storm and never seen again.

The adventurers — human, animal and insect — didn't succeed in crossing the Atlantic, but they did break the world's record for the longest flight. In recognition of their triumph, who should get his picture in the papers all across the world? Pudding, aka "Kiddo." And who should be holding him in the famous photograph cut out and pasted in so many young adventurers' scrapbooks?

A smiling Mr. Vaniman, who now saw the point of a cat.

When the Royal Mail ship docked in New York City, the crew and their cat were welcomed as heroes. Pudding spent a week in a gilt cage in the big bright window of Gimbels department store on 34th Street. You can guess how he felt about that, curled up with his paws over his eyes, crowds streaming by, tapping on the glass.

The flea protested. The noise! The humiliation of being put on display! Though the food was good and Pudding's blood not so sardiney, he didn't care. Pudding was wretched in this prison. The flea couldn't be happy now if his host wasn't.

"Let us out of here!" he shouted at the crowd, waving four unseeable fists.

But the outraged flea could only groan when he saw a familiar planet-sized face pressed against the window.

"Kitty! Oh, Kitty!"

"Cripes!" the flea said. "Her again!"

6
RMS TITANIC
1912
16

Pudding Tat did cross the Atlantic — by steamship. He came in the gilt cage he'd suffered inside in the window of Gimbels department store. For the next two years Edith Wellman and her four older sisters went to a London finishing school to learn how to be proper ladies. Proper ladies danced, played the piano and spoke French. They walked with books balanced on their heads. No one explained to them why they needed that particular skill, but they mastered it.

During these years Pudding was condemned to be an inside cat, though he was desperate to be out adventuring again. He knew he was far from home. So wouldn't he be near one of those four corners of the wide world?

The flea neither encouraged nor discouraged his host. His job now was to keep him out of trouble. Any pretty sound would draw him foolishly on. Without the flea's help, Pudding would surely be trampled, run over or drowned before too long.

In London, the main peril lay in the personage of Edith Wellman.

"Here she comes now," said the flea. "Run!"

The house, antiqued and brocaded, not far from Kensington Gardens, was finer even than Vincent Bryan's uptown apartment. Pudding was well fed on plate scrapings of mutton and beef that pleasantly flavored his blood. Yet the flea never over-indulged now. He drank when he needed and always stopped when he was full. Otherwise, who would look out for his host?

In April, the Wellmans booked a passage on the RMS *Titanic* and began packing up their many trunks. Home to New York City!

The morning they left England, a steward carried Pudding Tat in the Gimbels department store cage up the Grand Staircase and under the glass-domed ceiling. Though Pudding saw none of the grandeur of the ship, he smelled its paint-and-varnish newness. He heard the excited squeals of the five Wellman girls as they deposited the cage in their cabin.

"Let's go swimming," the next-youngest-to-Edith suggested.

"I'm going down to the engine room," Edith declared.

"You are *not!*"

"I am! I'm going to help shovel the coal."

The door slammed. From his gilt prison, Pudding

squinted around at the oak-paneled walls. He felt as miserable as Bostock's lion.

"Do something," the flea said. "You'll feel better. Have a wash. Your coat is looking tatty."

Pudding curled into a glum ball.

"Hey! Don't go to sleep! Let's put our heads together. Something will happen. When hasn't it?"

This is perfectly true. Every moment something happens, though it isn't always the something you're expecting.

At dinner, Mrs. Wellman and her daughters shared a table with an elderly American couple, Isador and Ida Straus, also from New York City. Isador was bald except for a cropped white fringe around his ears and a pointed white beard. Expressive black eyebrows danced above his spectacle rims. Plump Ida let him do most of the talking.

"Five sturdy daughters you have there," he told Mrs. Wellman. "My compliments."

"They were at school in England," she said. "And what's your line of work, Mr. Straus?"

"You've heard of Macy's?" Ida asked.

"Macy's!" Edith shrieked. "Gimbels is better!"

The two department stores, fierce rivals, stood across from each other on 34th Street.

Isador peered at Edith through his gold-rimmed spectacles and gave her a pretend frown. "My dear little girl. I own Macy's."

"Edith," chided her mortified sisters, who had actually learned some manners at finishing school. "Macy's is wonderful."

"But Kitty lived in the window in Gimbels."

Everyone knew about the explorer Walter Wellman. The astonished owner of Macy's said, "Your Kitty is the airship cat?"

The consommé arrived in china bowls. Isador passed around the basket of rolls.

"So you're the explorer's family? What an honor to be dining with you. An honor despite your preference for Mr. Gimbel."

"I'm sorry she offended you," said Mrs. Wellman, who had spoken these words countless times.

Isador winked at Edith. "An introduction to this famous cat will probably erase the insult."

After dinner, the Strauses visited the girls' cabin where the celebrity cat was curled up in the golden cage, his face concealed by his tail.

"He has the prettiest eyes," Edith told them. "I'll show you."

The old couple cringed as the girl dragged the cat out by the collar and forced open his eyes. Pudding writhed in pain. Isador glanced at Ida. She was biting her tongue.

"See?" Edith said.

"Yes," Ida told her, gently pulling away the girl's hand.

"And you keep him in this cage always?" Isador asked.

Just for the passage, Mrs. Wellman assured them. With all the activities on board it was unlikely they'd be in their cabin much. They couldn't let the cat roam free, for he was continually trying to escape.

The Strauses weren't interested in dancing in the ballroom or swimming in the saltwater pool. Squash and billiards held no attraction for them. In fact, none of the recreations available to the First Class passengers on the world's most luxurious ocean liner tempted them. They had each other.

"We'd be happy to keep him for the passage," Ida said. "Our stateroom is just down the hall. You can pop in to visit him."

"That's a wonderful idea," Mrs. Wellman said. "What do you think, Edith?"

But Edith had already run off.

So the Strauses took charge of the cat, and they all parted happily. Mrs. Wellman, especially. Now the girls could take full advantage of the opportunities the ship offered to practice their expensive new manners on wealthy bachelors.

Every evening after that, Isador and Ida ordered dinner in their room, keeping their feline guest in mind. Roast duckling or sirloin of beef?

"Sirloin!" the flea piped up.

Pudding purred louder when it appeared on the plate. For the pleasure of his flea.

After dinner, Isador enjoyed a cigar while the white lapful of cat dozed.

"*Ketsele?* Mr. Gimbel, my competitor, kept you in a cage. But if you come to Macy's, you'll be free. I invite you to visit our linen department. Find a cushion to your liking. Sleep as long as you want."

Ida rolled her stockings down over her swollen ankles. "Tell him about the Society."

"We have a mutual aid society," Isador explained to Pudding. "Any Macy's man or woman? Should something happen to him or her — God forbid — Macy's will help. We're in this world together, are we not? *Tzedakah* is our duty."

He paused to puff the cigar.

Ida pushed the ashtray closer to her husband. "But, Izzy? Does the cat understand Yiddish?"

"Ah!" Isador said. "As usual, you're right, my Ida, my bright Ida, my electric light bulb."

Stroking the cat, he switched to English. "Kitty? Do you understand?"

Pudding purred louder.

"He gets the gist," Isador told Ida.

All Pudding understood was that he was free of Edith and out of the cage. At night while the Strauses snored in their beds, he paced the lavish stateroom waiting for the moment when one of the Strauses, or their maid, would forget he was there and open the door. For now two oak-paneled bedrooms, a marbled bathroom and the parlor comprised his territory. The only reminder that he was on a ship came from the faraway throb of the engines powered by eight hundred tons of coal a day shoveled non-stop by two hundred men.

Under that mechanical throb he heard an orchestra like at the Pan-American Exposition. Several times a day it played, all together in after-dinner concerts, or as a quintet at teatime in the Café Parisien. A piano and a flock of strings — violins, cellos, a bass.

Such a pure sound after the crackling of the gramophone. If only he could get closer to it!

Four days into the voyage, Pudding's sensitive ears picked up a different sound — metal pierced, then ripping.

The great ship juddered.

"What was that?" the flea asked.

The Strauses slept on. Pudding continued to prowl. Soon he noticed something peculiar underfoot. The floor was tilting.

Not much later, the panicked maid pounded on the door. "Sir! Ma'am! I'm sorry to wake you, but it seems that we're evacuating the ship."

"It can't be sinking," Isador called. "This is the *Titanic*. The papers said it was unsinkable."

"Sir, you're supposed to gather on deck and only bring what you can carry in your pockets."

The old couple lumbered out of their beds.

Then Isador remembered. "Where's the cat?"

The corridor thronged with frightened passengers.

"Feet everywhere," the flea shouted. "Keep to the wall."

Pudding hurried along, unseeing and unseen. Somewhere beyond the hubbub he could hear the orchestra playing again. Through the tangle of panicking feet, the notes drew him on.

Out on the angled deck was where he found them, eight heroic men calmly gliding their bows.

Cranks squealed as the lifeboats were lowered into the darkness. Pursers shouted commands. "Women and children first! Line up here!"

The flea quailed. "You gotta listen to me, buddy, if we're going to get out of this one."

Pudding heard only those clear sorrowful notes.

The Strauses stepped on deck clutching each other, led by their terrified maid.

"But the cat," Isador was muttering. "We promised to take care of him. I'll go back."

A purser shouted, "Come on! Lively now! Women and children!"

"Mrs. Straus," the maid begged.

"Not without Isador. I will not be separated from my husband."

"But we're sinking, ma'am!"

Ida removed her fur coat and held it out to the maid. "You'll be cold."

The girl took it. Sobbing, she stumbled for the lifeboat.

Pudding heard a shot ring out. It broke the music's spell. He remembered that long-ago sound, the bitter odor, and shrank down in fear. Yet when he opened his eyes, he saw a beautiful sight — above him, a thousand stars exploding.

It was a flare gun. The Strauses, too, watched the shower of light. Nearby the orchestra was playing a dreamy song.

"Everyone's getting in that boat," the flea told Pudding.

Pudding said, "Let's listen for a few minutes."

"There aren't going to be any minutes left."

Isador heard mewing. When he looked down, the white cat was sitting peacefully at his feet.

"There you are!"

He took Ida's warm hand in his and kissed it. "Light of my life. My electric light bulb. Tell me, do you see the cat, too, or am I dreaming him?"

"All the blackness?" the flea told his host. "That's water."

At the dreaded word, Pudding snapped to. By then the great ship had begun to tip.

The end came with a horrifying racket. Baggage, coal, furniture, passengers and crew — everything and everyone slid toward the bow. Half-in and half-out of the water, the *Titanic* paused with her great propeller tilted to the stars.

With hundreds still clinging to the rails, the ship hovered between two worlds — water and air, death and life. Then, in one terrible, graceful motion, the *Titanic* slipped beneath the waves.

Pudding plunged into the hated water. Instinctively he kicked his legs until he burst back into the air. In the blackness, his eyes stinging from the salt, he swam on. Groans and ghostly pleas sounded all around him, the last cries of people soon to be ghosts themselves.

"Atta boy," the flea called like a tiny, parasitical coxswain. "Now swim! Swim!"

They wouldn't survive long in this cold. Many of the bodies bobbing around them, held afloat by cork life vests, were already corpses.

Beyond this frightening flotsam, they made out a familiar shape. A lifeboat, like the one they'd soared the skies in.

"Boat straight on," the flea directed.

Up ahead, a baby was crying. Pudding set out for that voice, noisily alive.

There were so many crammed into Lifeboat 16 that some, like Violet Jessop, had to stand. She was jiggling a howling baby in her arms — whose she didn't know. The purser had thrust him at her just before the boat was lowered. What a fracas on deck at the last minute! Wild-eyed men rushing to get on, threatening to tip them and spill them into the black ocean. An officer waved a gun and they backed off.

"Hush, baby, hush," she whispered to the child.

This lost infant wasn't the only terrified one. The boat was filled with women and children, a handful of crew who were working the oars, and Violet and two other stewardesses. The men pulled the oars, yelling to each other.

"Row! Get clear of the ship or we'll be sucked under with her!"

Violet offered the baby a finger to suck. It stopped crying at once, which only meant they better heard the thunderous smashing from the tipping ship and the screams of those still clinging to it.

The rowers slowed. A chilling silence fell upon them now.

Soon flotsam began drifting past — a suitcase, a violin, a chair — lit only by the hopeless glints of the stars. Several women began to cry again, but quietly now, for everyone in Lifeboat 16 knew that they had got out with their lives when so many others hadn't.

At least for now.

Then something small and pale caught Violet's eye. Fearing another lost baby, she asked a woman to take the whimpering one she held, another to hold her skirt while she leaned over the side.

"Miss!" one of the oarsmen shouted. "Don't do that!"

Ignoring him, she lifted Pudding by a hind leg.

"A cat," the oarsman said. "He's dead. Throw him back."

Years ago, when Violet was a little girl, her family had left their native Ireland for Argentina. On that crossing she had been very ill. No doctor on board, they hadn't expected her to survive. The captain had tended to her. All he had for medicine was a song.

She'd remembered that song her whole life.

Rocked in the cradle of the deep
I lay me down in peace to sleep;
Secure I rest upon the wave,
For thou, O Lord, hast power to save.

Violet looked down just as the sodden cat stirred in her arms.

"Look!" she cried. "He's alive."

"It's a sign!" one of the other women gasped.

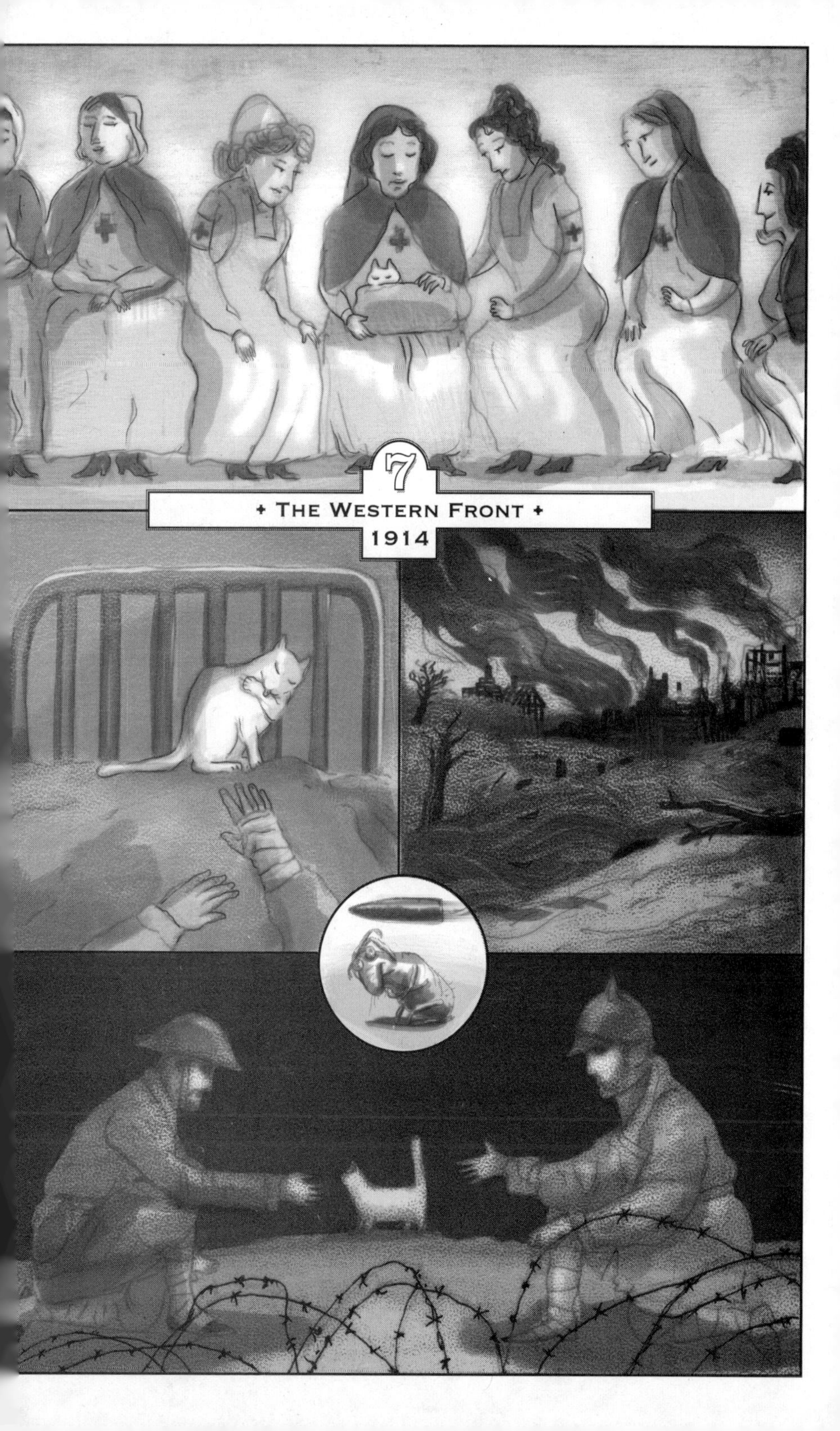
7
+ THE WESTERN FRONT +
1914

More than fifteen hundred perished when the *Titanic* sank, including Ida and Isador Straus and the eight musicians of the White Star Line Orchestra who had valiantly played until the very last moment. The survivors numbered just over seven hundred.

Hours after the tragedy, another ship, the *Carpathia*, arrived to rescue those in the lifeboats and transport them to New York. The few crew left alive were offered a return passage to England.

Violet had lost everything in the sinking, so she wasn't about to part with the cat. She took him to England and left him with her mother while she went on working as a stewardess.

In the house in Ealing, Pudding could safely come and go as he pleased, thanks to the flea, who warned him when an electric tram was passing on Uxbridge Road, or when a fox appeared on the commons green.

But Pudding didn't stray as far, or as often, as he had in the past. The electric lights that now lined the streets bothered his eyes. Also, Ealing was crowded with cats. All of them had staked a territory and would shred fur to defend it. Why accidentally trespass when mice were plentiful in Mrs. Jessop's garden?

Also, he was growing old. His bones seemed to ache more and more.

The flea didn't want Pudding anywhere near those Ealing cats either, or their mooching fleas.

"Back off," he'd say when an interloper hatched in the grass and came pronking over to catch a ride. "This is my host. Find yourself some other *Felis domesticus*."

There he would perch in Pudding's ear, preening his shaggy mouthparts, feeling very satisfied with his life, while Pudding enjoyed another long, long nap.

If Pudding was growing old, his flea was ancient. Back on the Willoughby farm, none of his brothers and sisters were still singing and dancing. He'd outlived them all.

While Pudding napped, he dreamed. In his dreams, he often found himself blinking into blackness. The blackness he'd seen beyond the edge of the hayloft in the barn. The blackness of the inside of a barrel. The blackness all around the *Titanic*'s sloping deck.

What it meant, he didn't know. Whenever he woke from these troubling dreams, he found himself longing for home.

All this time the wide world was changing still, but not fast enough anymore. Mrs. Jessop hosted suffragette meetings in her parlor, which often drove Pudding from his favorite napping spot on the divan. Women wanted the right to vote just like men. They were marching in the streets and hunger-striking for it.

And it wasn't just women. All over, people were growing restless with their old rulers and kings. In Europe, alliances were shifting, borders moving. Armies began gathering. Dark clouds floated closer.

Storm! Storm! Storm!

When Violet next got home to London, anxious to see her dear white cat, her mother met her at the door in tears.

"Have you heard, Vi?" she cried. "We're at war!"

Violet knew what she had to do. She signed up with the Voluntary Aid Detachment as a junior nurse. Within two weeks she was on a ship bound for Belgium with a giddy group of new nurses.

"I'll be back for Christmas," she told her mother when she left.

All the nurses believed this.

"Absence makes the heart grow fonder anyway, don't it?" one said. She took a photograph out of her bag and passed it around. "This is my Jimmy. He's in France. Having a great time, I'm sure!"

"Dashing! How about you, Vi? Do you have a sweetheart?"

"I do." Violet patted the bag in her lap.

"Let's see his picture."

Violet clutched the bag to her chest. She was having misgivings about what she'd done, but like the others were saying, it was only for a month or two. Then they'd be back home.

She unzipped the bag and let them have a peek. Pudding squinted up at the women's surprised faces.

"A cat!"

Violet put a finger to her lips. "I couldn't bear to part with him again. He was with me through the darkest hours of my life."

They decided that Pudding would be their mascot. After they docked and the cavalcade of motorcars arrived to transport them to the hospital in Antwerp, they had their first chance to show him off. In every village they drove through, people lined the road, calling, "*Vive la Croix-Rouge!* Long live the Red Cross!"

Violet would lift Pudding out of the bag and hold him up for the villagers to see.

"*Vive le chat!*" they shouted, waving their hats in the air. "Long live the cat!"

"Listen to them shouting to you!" the flea gloated.

Pudding shut his eyes tighter. He smelled blood in the air — human, not mouse.

Later, the cavalcade passed a line of mud-spackled soldiers marching grimly along the roadside. These men didn't look up, only limped along staring at the ground.

The nurses stopped laughing. Violet slipped the cat back into her bag. They traveled the rest of the way in an uneasy silence.

The hospital was in an evacuated palace. No sooner had Violet been assigned a bunk than she was ordered down a marble staircase to a long ballroom where seventy beds stood side by side, all filled with groaning soldiers. She and one other nurse just as inexperienced as she had to care for all these wounded. Sometimes all they could offer to relieve the men's pain was the hem of a sheet to clench between their teeth.

With the work and the suffering, Violet barely thought of Pudding over those months. She simply left the door to her room ajar so he could roam.

Roam he did. Pudding padded through the once-elegant rooms in this palace of misery.

"This is awful," the flea said. "Anywhere is better than here. Let's go."

Pudding prowled on, restless, uneasy, as though in one of his own foreboding dreams.

Violet sat beside a feverish French soldier whose left leg had been blown off. Every night she sat this vigil, for he told her it helped him endure his agony to have her near.

The night the soldier died, Violet heard him muttering as she mopped his brow.

"Ange, ange."

She leaned closer. He pointed with a bandaged hand and Violet turned.

There, on the foot of the bed, her white angel of a cat sat blinking in the darkness.

In December, Violet was transferred to a hospital closer to the Front. From the back of the motorcar, she stared out at the ruined countryside, the trenches scarring the muddy fields, the tangled bales of barbed wire. The villages were deserted, their churches blasted to rubble, the colored glass from their windows scattered.

"Why?" she asked out loud.

"Why what?" answered the soldier who was driving her.

"Why are we fighting?"

The man snorted. "Because somebody we never heard of shot somebody else we never heard of in a place we never heard of. It's called war."

"It's terrible."

"Truer words were never spoken, miss."

The makeshift hospital was in an old stone farmhouse that shook with the continuous roar of guns. Pudding huddled under Violet's cot in the attic where all the nurses slept in one large cold room — when they could sleep. Every blast shook the walls. Pudding's nostrils filled with the scent of death.

The flea whimpered. "That sound."

Along with the hammering of the shells came the rumble of the ambulances that delivered stretchers full of wounded and carried off the dead. When Pudding ventured out — which he did as seldom as possible — he asked the flea what he saw.

"Mud. It just goes on and on."

Less than a mile away, John Willoughby was standing knee-deep in muck at the bottom of a trench. It had been four months since he'd joined up. He was a Canadian with a scholarship to study at Oxford, the world's finest university. Just a farm boy from Welland County. Little Johnny Willoughby, a scholar! His parents were bursting with pride.

But the war broke out before he even opened a book. Off he raced, hoping for adventure. He'd dress up in khaki, blast a rifle, march. Every night they'd hit the pubs. By Christmas, he'd be back in school.

Well, it *was* Christmas, and instead he was freezing in this hole in the ground with a tin hat on his head. He wouldn't make it out alive. But if he did? If he survived? He was going home. Forget Oxford. He'd already got more education than he could ever use.

His first day in the trenches, the man beside him got shot in the neck. Lesson: keep your head down. Two weeks in, his feet started to rot in his boots. Lesson: dry your feet every night or you'll lose your toes to trench rot.

Lately, he'd been crying for no reason. Lesson: nobody cares how you feel.

Oh, yes. He was educated now.

The soldier next to him shimmied up the wall of sandbags and peeked over the top of the trench, trying to see where the enemy was positioned. A shot whizzed by.

"Merry Christmas to you, too!" John shouted.

Of course the German soldier who'd fired the shot was himself huddled miserably in his wet trench on the other side of No Man's Land. This is what got to John. Whoever was over there probably only wanted to be home for Christmas, too. Warm and safe and dry with people who loved him rather than people who were trying to kill him.

Why *was* John trying to kill him? Why was that German trying to kill John? Who knew?

"I forgot it was Christmas," said the soldier beside him in the trench. "Do you think they'll give us pudding in our rations or just the same old muck?"

John turned away, tears in his eyes. His mother always made pudding at Christmas, and afterward John's father took a bowl of it to the barn for the cats. The sweetness of that memory made his present circumstances unbearable. He was going to cry again if he didn't do something else.

"Let's have a carol."

His trench mate scoffed, but John sang anyway. He started with "Silent Night." His mate grinned then and joined in, prompting the other soldiers along the muddy line to turn and look.

At that moment, Pudding was creeping along the burned fringe of trees, having walked out that morning. He'd thought of something in the night. Maybe there were no corners. If there weren't, all he had to do was keep walking in a straight line. Then he'd be home.

Pudding heard the singing then — one clear voice at first, then others joining in and gathering force under the ringing bullets.

"Whoa!" said the flea as they stepped into No Man's Land. "Hold on! Stop!"

On the German side, some of the soldiers had heard the carol, too, and shouted for their gunners to cease. They knew the song as "Stille Nacht." One soldier volunteered to peek over the top of the trench. When he clambered back down, his expression was so strange that the others leaned their weapons against the sandbags and climbed up to look for themselves.

Pudding, drawn by the music, stepped delicately into the broad stretch of horror.

"Far enough!" the flea said. "Buddy, you are lucky you can't see this."

Nothing grew around the charred tree trunks and the mortar craters filled with oily water. Several dead soldiers lay twisted in the mud, German and British. Walking through this desolation, carefully skirting the water, was a pure white cat so utterly calm that his eyes were closed.

The German stared at the white cat with its tail raised high. A living flag proclaiming a truce on this day of peace.

On the British side, John volunteered to find out why the firing had stopped.

"Careful, Willoughby," someone said. "It's probably a trick."

John looked over the trench. He saw forty or more German heads with their curious spiked helmets looking back at him.

No, they were looking at something in the middle of No Man's Land. And all of them were singing.

"Eine Katze!" one of the Germans called across to him.

A cat. It was almost the same word in English. There it was, a small white cat with muddied legs, stepping lightly through this hell.

A memory flooded back. John must have been about five. An albino kitten had been born on the farm. It was the only kitten that he ever got near enough to touch. One day it dashed out of the barn and was never seen again.

Cat and *Katze*. The carol was the same, too. So why were they trying to kill each other? And what was that cat doing out there where it would be blown to bits?

John did something then that surprised even himself. The night before, one of their brigade had tried to enter the No Man's Land to collect a body. He, too, was shot. Now two of their men lay there.

John wasn't going to see that innocent animal hurt on Christmas Eve. They could shoot him first if they wanted. He heaved himself over the top of the trench. On both sides the singing stopped. It hadn't been this quiet for months.

As John walked toward the cat, the eyes of two armies followed his every step. When he got close enough, he crouched.

"Here, kitty. Here, kitty."

"Turn back," the flea roared. "Don't listen to him."

But there was something in the cadence of that friendly voice that sounded familiar to Pudding. He rushed right to him and rubbed himself against John's leg.

"Heads up, Johnny!" someone shouted.

A German soldier came sidling over. He didn't seem to be armed. He, too, crouched down and John saw that he was young.

John had never seen a German this close. Not a live one, anyway.

Shyly, the German boy smiled and said, "Merry Christmas."

His accent was so funny that John threw back his head and laughed.

From this place on Christmas Eve, 1914, peace spread all down the Western Front. Within hours, two entire armies had climbed out of their miserable ditches, crossed over, and shaken hands.

John shook the German boy's. "I wish I had a present to give you," he said.

He patted the pockets of his trench coat. Nothing but a pad and pencil, his pocket knife, a picture of his mother.

And buttons! He tore one off his coat and offered it to the soldier, who did the same. A brass reminder of the German he didn't kill.

He would keep it all his life.

Out of nowhere a soccer ball came flying and a jubilant cry rose up. Two pairs of helmets became the goalposts, spiked German ones on one side, domed British ones on the other. John and the German watched the game, the cat purring in John's arms. Then John took the damp pad from his pocket. He wrote, *John Willoughby, Welland County, Ontario, Canada,* tore the page out and gave it to the German.

"Write to me when this is all over, brother. Write to me if you're alive."

Christmas Day, 1914, Private John Willoughby woke from a doze in his dugout in a Saint-Yves trench. The night before he'd made a bed for the cat, but now the animal was gone.

It had rained in the night and the water was even deeper in the trench. He doubted a blind cat would get far in these conditions, and he was right. When he looked up, he saw the cat sitting at the top of the trench in full view of the Germans, washing himself.

John climbed up and, appearing over the top, opened his arms to scoop up the cat.

How miniscule a flea is! Things we can't see are quite visible to them. Small things seem huge, no matter how fast they're moving.

The flea heard a whine and then some strange code from the past echoed in his head: *Dah di dah di, dah dah di dah, dah di di.*

A bullet.

"Duck!!!" he screamed in Pudding's ear.

And Pudding listened.

The blow sent John flying backward. Pain bloomed like a poppy across his chest.

Violet Jessop was heart-broken when the ambulance brought in this last load of wounded. Among them was her own cat, bloodied and tucked in beside a soldier with a shoulder wound.

She laid the cat in an empty crate and pushed it into a corner to give him a proper burial later. She didn't cry. So many men had died, she had no tears left.

The next time she looked, the cat was gone. She assumed someone had disposed of the body, but when she checked on Private Willoughby, there he was, curled up asleep at the wounded soldier's feet.

"How did he end up with you?" she asked when John was conscious again and recovering from surgery.

John told her of the cat's mysterious appearance the day before. He described the last moment he remembered, just before he was shot. How he'd raised himself over the edge of the trench.

"He was in your arms when it happened?"

"I believe so," John said.

"Well, judging from your wound, I'd say he spared you from having your whole shoulder blown off. If that had happened, you would have bled to death."

8
WELLAND COUNTY, ONTARIO, CANADA
1915

Mrs. Willoughby fussed at the woodstove. She couldn't stop cooking for Johnny. Oatmeal with fresh cream, griddle cakes, back bacon, applesauce. Just baked bread! A young man needed his own mother's cooking to heal. That's what she believed and so had been standing at this stove ever since Johnny got home from the war.

Farmer Willoughby came downstairs and poured himself a cup of tea.

"How is he?" she asked.

"Sleeping. Nice color to his face. Won't be long till he's up and around."

Because of my griddle cakes, Mrs. Willoughby thought but didn't say. When she turned, she saw a peculiar expression on her husband's face.

"Is he still talking in his sleep, the poor lad?" she asked him.

Farmer Willoughby nodded. "Keeps muttering about the cat."

The blind white cat Johnny had brought home from France. Some nurse had given it to him. The hospital mascot turned hospital ship mascot. Johnny believed it had saved his life.

"It's the shell shock," Mrs. Willoughby said, shaking her head. "He never should have left home. I was against it. I told you so. Oxford? Bah!"

"He'll get up. He's strong. Then he'll be off again. There's a whole world out there. He should see it. Home will always be here for him."

Mrs. Willoughby sniffed and kept on stirring. He was right, but it was a mother's job to worry.

"His porridge is nearly ready," she finally said. "Would you bring up some cream?"

Farmer Willoughby rose from the table, pausing to take a last swig of tea.

"Do you remember Old Puddy had an albino kitten once? Years back now."

"She's had a hundred kittens."

"But you don't forget one like that. And it was blind too. I distinctly remember it."

Just then the cat appeared in the kitchen doorway as though he'd heard them talking about him.

"And there's the very fellow!" Farmer Willoughby cried.

Mrs. Willoughby glanced at the cat. They'd never allowed an animal in the house before, had certainly never let one sleep in a bed. But the cat had stationed himself at the foot of Johnny's, as though guarding him. It didn't seem hygienic. Fleas and whatnot.

She had to admit, though, that Johnny had improved more rapidly than the doctors had predicted while under the cat's watch.

Watch? What was she talking about? The creature was blind.

Farmer Willoughby made a clicking noise. The cat came and wove himself around his legs, meowing. Then he found the kitchen wall and followed it until he reached the back door. There he sat on the mat with his eyes closed. Waiting.

"I suppose he'd like some breakfast, too," Mrs. Willoughby said. "Go get that cream."

Farmer Willoughby lifted his winter coat off the hook by the door, bundled himself up and stepped out.

And Pudding Tat walked out with him. The bright sun glittered on the snow, so he kept his eyes shut tight and listened to the flea's directions.

"Straight on. He's stomped out a path there. Now giddy-up because he's opened the barn door. He'll close it in a second."

Pudding heard the squawking hinges and made a dash for it.

The rhythmic munching of cud, the quiet huff of the cow as her milk rang out in the metal pail. The buzz-huff-hum-twitter-thrum-scratch-squeak. The purr-mew-nicker-clank. The sweetest music in the wide world.

And the smells! Hay and the blood of living things. Mice and horses and cows.

And one cat — Mother Tat.

Farmer Willoughby sat on his stool. As he bent over his pail, Pudding leapt onto his shoulder.

"Hey!" He laughed. He would swear the cat knew where he was going.

Of course he did! Up in the loft Old Puddy was mewing.

From the farmer's back, Pudding made it to the top of the milking stall. From the milking stall, to the shelf. There he crouched, aiming for the loft.

Then he sailed. Sailed through the air.

up!
up,
up,
Up,
Home.

AUTHOR'S NOTE

I lied. This story isn't "mostly" true. It's more like "somewhat" true. Though my original intention in writing this novel was to accurately represent certain historical events, the literal truth kept getting in the way of the "story truth." Also, making things up is so much fun.

Nevertheless, I'd like to encourage you, dear reader, to investigate further the real people who appear in these pages.

Annie Edson Taylor was indeed the first person to ride over Niagara Falls in a barrel. A cat was involved in the stunt, but versions of the story vary. Some report that the cat was sent down the falls ahead of time as a test. It survived. Annie's manager, Frank M. Russell, really did steal the barrel. Annie spent most of her savings hiring a private detective to try to get it back. She died, penniless, at the age of eighty-two.

Asa Philip is a made-up character based on the many African American railway porters who worked in unfair, discriminatory conditions for the Pullman Company. I named him after Asa Philip Randoph, who organized the Brotherhood of Sleeping Car Porters in 1925, the first African American labor union in the United States. A. Philip Randolph would only have been twelve years old in 1901.

Giancarlo Casali is also a made-up character. Like him, many thousands of child street musicians were sent from Italy to London, Paris and New York as indentured laborers in the nineteenth century.

President McKinley was shot in the Temple of Music at the Pan-American Exposition on September 6, 1901. He died eight days later. Here is a place where "story truth" took precedence over history. Annie Edson Taylor performed her feat on October 24th of that year, *after* the assassination, not before.

Vincent Bryan and Gus Edwards are real. Both went on to have successful careers, Vincent Bryan in Hollywood.

Jack Irwin was the first person in history to send an air-to-land telegraph message. The crew of the *America* truly did not know if sending that message would cause an explosion.

And there really was a stowaway cat aboard, a tabby called Kiddo, whom they did try to lower onto the tugboat. After the aborted flight, Kiddo was displayed in the window of Gimbels department store. He then went to live with Edith Wellman, who was probably a very nice person, unlike the Edith in this book.

The Wellmans were not on the *Titanic* when it sank, but Isador and Ida Straus were. Ida could have got into a lifeboat and saved herself, but she refused to part from her husband. Isador was so beloved by the employees of Macy's that they used their own money to create a memorial plaque to him and Ida. You can ask to see it in the 34th Street Macy's in New York City.

Violet Jessop was a stewardess on the *Titanic* who did later serve as a nurse with the British Red Cross in World War I. However, she worked on a hospital ship, not on the Western Front. She actually survived a second sinking, in 1916, of the ship *Britannic*.

Johnny Willoughby is imaginary. However, more than 619,000 real Canadians enlisted to fight in World War I. Approximately 424,000 served overseas and 59,544 died.

The Christmas Truce of 1914 is true. There are no records of a white cat instigating it, but why not?

Most fleas only live about two or three months, but this is because they are blood-sucking parasites. Helping others has been scientifically proven to decrease stress, anxiety, depression, blood pressure and the likelihood of dying early.

Speaking of helping others, I gratefully acknowledge the financial support of the Canada Council for the Arts in writing this book, as well as the moral and literary support of my tireless editor, Shelley Tanaka, and the person to whom this book is dedicated, the irreplaceable Sheila Barry.

PUDDING TAT'S PLAYLIST

"The Ballad of the Thirsty Flea" and "The Bloodless Flea's Lament," traditional flea songs (not discernible to human ears)

"I Love You Truly" (1901), music and lyrics by Carrie Jacobs-Bond

"When the Train Comes Along," a traditional African American spiritual

"La Biondina in gondoleta," a traditional Venetian song

Organ Sonatas (1727-30), Johann Sebastian Bach

"In My Merry Oldsmobile" (1905), music by Gus Edwards, lyrics by Vincent P. Bryan

"That Beautiful Rag" (1910), music by Ted Snyder, lyrics by Irving Berlin.

"Dream of Autumn" (1908), music and lyrics by Archibald Joyce

"Rocked in the Cradle of the Deep" (1853), music by Joseph P. White, lyrics by Emma C. Willard

"Silent Night, Holy Night"/ "Stille Nacht, heilige Nacht" (1818), Franz Xaver Gruber, lyrics by Joseph Mohr (German) / John Freeman Young (English)

CAROLINE ADDERSON is an award-winning author of books for children and adults. Her work for adults has been nominated for the International IMPAC Dublin Literary Award, two Commonwealth Writers' Prizes, the Scotiabank Giller Prize, the Governor General's Literary Award and the Rogers Writers' Trust Fiction Prize. Her middle-grade novel, *Middle of Nowhere*, won the Sheila E. Egoff Children's Literature Prize and was shortlisted for the CLA Children's Book of the Year Award. She is also the author of the enormously successful Jasper John Dooley series.

Caroline is program director of the Writing Studio at the Banff Centre for Arts and Creativity. She lives in Vancouver.